I0578663

Reckoning 5
Print Edition: Summer 2021
Poetry Editor: Leah Bobet
Prose Editor: Cécile Cristofari

Reckoning *is a communal effort.*
Editorial staff, in alphabetical order:

Noa Covo
Michael J. DeLuca
Danika Dinsmore
Mohammad Shafiqul Islam
Andrew Kozma
Giselle K. Leeb
Johannes Punkt
Waverly SM
Aïcha Martine Thiam
Hal Y. Zhang

Cover and text ornament by Hana Amani

Reckoning Press
206 East Flint Street
Lake Orion, MI 48362
www.reckoning.press
distributed by IngramSpark
printed by Book Mobile
on 100% post-consumer recyled paper.

Reckoning 5

Contents

Cover
Reckoning 5

Hana Amani

HANA AMANI is a Sri Lankan visual artist and curator. Having received a Bachelor in Design from Emily Carr University of Art And Design, she lives in Vancouver, creating prints based on myth and folk-lore. With a love of art history and a curiosity about the future, Amani's work follows themes both of historical and futuristic concepts, with an emphasis on the state of women. She loves science fiction, opera, fairytales, playing chess, and listening to Amadeus at midnight. You can find more of her work on Instagram as hana.on.earth.

The Beach

From the Editors

Cécile Cristofari

Winter comes (in Provence, it looks much the same as summer from a distance, only crisp and windier), and with it the end of a long, harrowing year. A year of sorrow, for the families of a million and a half. A year of change, some say, though change may be less eagerly anticipated than a return to normal. An opportunity to take a break, for a lucky few, to think, to watch, to wonder. To realise that, no matter how sheltered, no one is safe from the brutal consequences of environmental destruction.

As I asked short story authors to share their sense of wonder with us, to stop and look at the world and report on the beauties they glimpsed there, I had no idea how relevant that question would be, a year later. Yet as the virus came to us out of destroyed forests and ravaged species, the question of the cost of sheltered lifestyles is more pressing than ever. How can we protect our environment if we are hardly ever reminded that it exists? Living in the heart of cities, it is far too easy to forget that there is such a thing as nature, messy, scary and uncontrollable, when trees around us are slashed into submission every year, weeds plucked out of pavements and birds driven out with spikes and hoses. Nature is no longer a fact of life, but a rumour, a holiday experience. Our lives have adjusted around its absence.

There are reports that as covid numbers soar, sales of scented candles drop, as customers report on their disappointing lack of smell. Whether it is true or not, the realisation gives one pause: we live in a world where it is plausible to imagine that thousands of people would fail to realise that they've lost one of their senses, so little do they use it in their lives. It is equally disturbing to hear the phrase 'augmented reality' used, without irony, to refer to games that restrict reality to pixels on a palm-sized screen. The enormity of the loss, when the reality itself of the world we live in, its weight, its sensorial presence, has faded away from our lives should no longer be allowed to go unnoticed.

But it would be far too easy to answer with nostalgia. There is no utopian past to go back to; we are the direct result of the centuries that preceded us, where nature was an enemy, a poison, an endless source of fear. We did not descend from a golden age. But maybe we can make it come true.

So let's make it happen. Let's head towards a world where the ground under our feet crawls with life, and we don't call it vermin. A world where glyphosate is only allowed to keep existing to rectify past mistakes, where trees grow free and rivers run clean, where the people who live off untamed forests and tundras no longer have to fight for dignity and peace, where the beasts that terrify us are left alone rather than slaughtered, when we turn the mistakes of our past into something that can thrive again.

This is a time of waiting, of stillness, but only if we accept it so.

When winter descends on Provence, the north wind sometimes turns the sky into the purest, brightest shade of blue. Such stillness can only come from the deepest turmoil, air twirling above in mighty currents, even though we cannot see it. Only when we look down to the ground do we notice the trees swaying. Only when we pause at last to look at what stands right in front of us do we realise that movement is in the nature of the world, and it only takes a strong will to steer it where we want it to go.

The present is clay, sitting cool and wet in the palm of your hand. Squash it, twist it, mold it. Shape it into something beautiful.

Cécile Cristofari lives in South France, where she teaches English to unruly but endearing teenagers. Her stories have previously appeared in *Daily Science Fiction*. In a previous life, she authored a PhD dissertation on imaginary cosmogonies in science fiction and fantasy (someone once described it as "more dedicated fan work than academic work," which she chooses to take as a compliment). She blogs at http://staywherepeoplesing.wordpress.com/.

From the Editors
a scribbled note in a water-damaged notebook

Leah Bobet

The call for submissions for *Reckoning 5*'s poetry started as a scribbled note in a water-damaged notebook I lost years ago. It was Toronto labour rights activist and scholar Dr. Winnie Ng's answer to a 2013 panel question on what she'd tell young organizers: that we can organize from rage, but where it was possible, you could go the long haul if you organized from joy. I lost the notebook, so I'm not going to get that quote right.

Living in a busy urban downtown sharpens your vision for the natural world living alongside and around you. You start relationships: with the raccoon that topples over your compost bin to eat tomato scraps; with the ash tree whose lowest leaves are low enough to, on the days you wear high heels to work, brush the top of your head like a benediction. You learn to truly value that ecosystem threaded through the cracks, and realize that busy spaces are full of half-visible mitzvot. You can think *nobody* is and then your vision sharpens to those little signs, and you realize: *somebody* is. That public native species garden didn't grow itself, and those squirrels aren't fat and happy on their own account. Someone planted chestnut trees. Someone is, just outside your frame of reference, doing the work.

Our call for poetry was about those intimacies: the seed waiting in your pocket, cupped handfuls of gorgeous things in motion, little gods. What work you were doing, and why you did it. Maybe we could all sharpen our vision, together.

We had no idea what was coming.

In Toronto, I have spent this pandemic year uneasily hibernating as part of a high-risk household. I stepped outside in May and the trees were leafing outward; the next time, in mid-June, the flowers were already going to fruit. It has been hard to know whose precautions to trust, where the future was leading.

Meanwhile, submissions poured in from every continent except Antarctica, and built a paper spine to keep my head up as the case counts fluctuated. Every week this year, I've spent a few hours reading poetry and essays about those little flecks of possibility: vivid, loving descriptions of the ground as wrinkled wise skin; laughing lines about coral; how far you can travel on patched-up sails; "we breathe and breathe and / breathe". Ambivalent, pragmatic, realistic, joyous, fierce, those carefully nurtured loves started to feel like sonar, describing the shape of a world latticed with *somebody is*. Everything was most-beautiful. Webbed between chat servers, databases, and international video calls scheduled delicately to link three time zones—systems that felt like they should be so tenuous—what's emerged is so solidly real.

Doing this project in a disrupted, unsettled year meant no matter what I could find to fear, *somebody is*. The process of putting this volume together gave us the proof. I can close my eyes and see a constellation: hundreds of people who believe in the limitless potential of being *for* something fiercely enough to write about it during a global pandemic.

That's what I hope this offers you: a volume that holds the proof, that shakes with the force of that jotted-down note seven years ago, organize from joy. Even though the notebook got soaked until it was unreadable, was lost in a move, and I had to dig through old websites and event listings to find the conference and rediscover Dr. Ng's name to properly credit her for the impact, I remembered the important part all the way through: *If I love things and work from that love, my strength will not fail me.*

So, here we are—not all of us, and not in equal circumstances: on our balconies, in wide-open spaces, in overcrowded housing with a half-dozen people we love, doing the work with our hands, doing the work with our mouths, holding ourselves or other people together, failing for today to do it, following instinct, following best practice, fumbling, planting, advocating, pushing back, pushing forward. Tending tiny miracles until they split the pavement.

Leah Bobet's most recent novel, *An Inheritance of Ashes,* won the Sunburst, Copper Cylinder, and Prix Aurora Awards. Her short fiction has appeared in multiple Year's Best anthologies, and her poetry in *Uncanny Magazine*, *Goblin Fruit*, and *Strange Horizons*. She lives and works in Toronto, where she contributes to food security and civic engagement projects and makes heroic amounts of jam. Visit her at www.leahbobet.com.

Salvage Song

Julia DaSilva

So, here we are
at the end.
We have pulled down the sails to make patches for the ocean, come
we will patch those patches with paisley scraps,
with blue and white checks like
Dorothy's dress, we will save scraps of paper
to cover half-written books; come we will grab
one last plank from the ship to patch
somewhere out past the epilogue. Come,
there is so much farther to go.

Let go of the ship's rope ladder, and we'll talk
about walking lightly on the world. Not
that we shouldn't have built the ship or made
the voyage, that the less anyone
could feel your wake, the better; not
some correspondence between the weight
of each step and the storm befalling us—but follow, step light,
if only because the raft is so easily tipped.
Step light down to the raft:
apply your whole self to the push and pull,
to the tumbling forward, the pause, and we will hop
from salvaging to salvaging.

Here at the end
you will feel you are doing nothing, and
you won't: when you think
about the space between
water droplets, a shortness of breath
will lodge in your chest the pain of knowing
there is so much to salvage, a folding
like reaching to tuck even the voyage
back into the pattern.

If you have no hope, you've come
to the right place to be hopeful
without it. And if you're worried
this is escape, I will assure
you: there is no escape.
We will drift
in the mess of an oceanic canal flush with pink
rhinestones from prom dates
that never happened and as we go
we will sew up the waves. When the raft sinks,
plug your nose, look up, and hold your breath
a little longer than comfortable. Your heartbeat
will pulse diamond in the water around you.
Take just enough with you
to swim back to the world.

So here at the end this song
is for drifting, this song
is for knowing your drifting goes somewhere, this song
is for pulling with all your might
against dead air. Out here,
you will have so much desire you will forget
how to have desires,
but that's okay, because this
is the end of the world
and we don't have new things.

And I don't mean to say
this couldn't be a love story.
Only that we'll have to salvage
from the love stories already written, here
at the end of the world.

Julia DaSilva's poetry has appeared in *Eclectica, Rat's Ass Review, Lychee Rind* zine, *Cathexis, Sapphic Writers Collective, Half A Grapefruit,* and the University of Toronto journals *The Spectatorial, The Strand,* and *Hardwire.* She is a guest in Tkaronto/Toronto on Dish With One Spoon territory, and writes fantasy as well as poetry, with a particular interest in the politics of magic systems. Her writing is informed by her work in climate justice organizing, and explores questions of political responsibility and queerness, embodiment, love and hope in worlds coming apart and being rebuilt.

Mula sa Melismas

Marlon Hacla

Bukod sa tubig, bukod sa paglalayag, mga pagpatay
at mga resulta ng pagbibilang ng hakbang,
pagsunod sa kapahamakan gayundin ang pagkilala
sa mga galaw na itinatago ng mga dayandang.
Malamig ang panahon para sa paglukso
sa mga konklusyon kung dumidistansiya
ba ang mga konstelasyon. Parang nauuso
na naman ang pagmimiron sa mga signos
ng pagbabalik ng Panginoon. Sabay-sabay
na naman ba ang pagposisyon, naglulusugan
ba ang mga puso ng mga bata, bumibilis
ba ang mga kabayo? Kung mag-iisip ba ako
ng mga ibon, lalabas ba ang mga ibon?
Kung mag-iisip ba ako ng kaluwalhatian,
lalabas ba ang mga mekanismo ng hangin,
papangalanan ba ang lahat ng klase
ng sugat upang ipaliwanag ang mga pinsala
sa paligid, upang linawin ang paglampas
ng tubig sa mga naitakdang hangganan
kung hangganan bang maituturing
ang mga lubid at tulos ng aking ligalig?

From Melismas

Marlon Hacla

Translated from Filipino by Kristine Ong Muslim

Aside from water, aside from sailing, killings
and results of counting steps,
in pursuit of danger as well as familiarity
of gestures shielded from view by dayandang trees.
The season's too cold for leaping
to conclusions on whether constellations are drifting farther
away from us. Doomsday cultists are coming out of the woodwork
these days, crowing about supposed signs
of the Second Coming. Do we now synchronize
our positions, are the children's hearts
getting healthier, are the horses
trotting faster than before? Suppose I imagine
birds, will that conjure birds?
If I visualize paradise,
will that render visible the wind's unseen machinery,
will that produce names for all kinds
of wounds to make plain the level of damage wrought
to the environment, to explain the water rise
going beyond the expected limits
assuming we can still consider as limits
the coiled ropes and upright pickets of my unease?

Marlon Hacla's first book, *May Mga Dumadaang Anghel sa Parang* (Manila: National Commission for Culture and the Arts, 2010), was published as part of UBOD New Authors Series II. His second book, *Glossolalia*, was published by High Chair in 2013. He also released two chapbooks, *Labing-anim na Liham ng Kataksilan* (2014) and *Melismas* (2016). He lives in Quezon City, Philippines, with his cats.

Kristine Ong Muslim is the author of nine books of fiction and poetry, including *The Drone Outside* (Eibonvale Press, 2017), *Black Arcadia* (University of the Philippines Press, 2017), *Meditations of a Beast* (Cornerstone Press, 2016), *Butterfly Dream* (Snuggly Books, 2016), *Age of Blight* (Unnamed Press, 2016), and *Lifeboat* (University of Santo Tomas Publishing House, 2015). She is also the translator of two bilingual volumes of Marlon Hacla's work: *Melismas* (Oomph Press, 2020) and *There Are Angels Walking the Fields* (forthcoming from Broken Sleep Books). Widely anthologized, Muslim's short stories have appeared in *Conjunctions*, *Dazed Digital*, and *World Literature Today*.

No More Creepy Crawlies

Anthony Pearce

There are no creepy crawlies hiding in my garden. I know, because I've checked.

The compost, under-turned and full of fresh scraps, should have attracted all manner of bugs and buzzers. The tree hanging overhead should be bowing down with orb weavers, feasting on the to-and-fro flitting parade. The bushes should be moving, rustling, going bump in the night as our insectivore friends come out to play.

There should be corpses. Nature is red in tooth and claw, and nothing lives forever. There should be bits, unglamorous chunks, remnants of private, unseen disputes as the hierarchy of predator and prey is reinforced. A feather, a tuft, a tail. There should be beetles and millipedes and worms, seething and swarming, biting and gnawing, beginning the process of making dirt from flesh.

Should be.

It's amazing what you see when you pay attention. Keep your head up, they say, as if the world below isn't stuffed to the brim with detail. In the great documentary of life, all the trailer snapshots might be happening in the trees and tall grass, but the meat-and-bones production work happens beneath our feet. The detail work, the foundations—the catering.

As a kid in the 'Lucky Country' of Australia, that was all I did: look down. Oh, sure, I looked up sometimes—birds and possums and spiderwebs all demand at least a little attention—but down below, things crawled. Spiders and hoppers scattered from leaf litter, careening off to safety from clumsy hands. The damp spaces under school demountables practically hoarded slugs, snails, frogs, and enough slime and gunk to definitively ruin a school uniform. Multicoloured ants swarmed the playground boundaries. The yellow-arsed ones taste like honey—honest! Go on, give it a try!

The trail up past my local golf course held so many lizards I ran out of memory on my tiny brick cellphone capturing them all in an afternoon. Christmas beetles invaded the damn living room every single summer, no matter what.

And always, always, there was the possibility of the unfiltered joy of a fistfull of dirt and the unearthing of something small, wriggling, and absolutely unsanitary.

I've lived just north of Sydney pretty much my entire life. I never moved away, and I never stopped digging. I think everything else might have moved, though.

When I dig into the ground now, I find more plastic debris than worms. Hell, I don't find any worms at all. We've got a few crawlers like the ever-dependable pillbug, but not much else. The joy I find in dirt is very much filtered.

I'm not really supposed to dig, of course—the strata and home-owners associations don't want to disrupt the neat, even, conformist rectangles of yellow-brown dying vegetation. I dig, though, keeping all the plastic I find in an unmarked bag in my tool cupboard. Couldn't really tell you why I keep it. The worry, maybe, that if I throw it all out it'll just end up in someone else's dirt.

We have rules and expectations, and they must be stuck to. No leaf litter. Dead grass, wilting in the summer heat as the dirt dries and roots burn, unshaded and unnourished by its blades cropped too short, far too short. No "untidy" native lawn, no "weeds", and absolutely no food crops. These are the rules and expectations. A system, designed from the ground up to sabotage itself across months and years.

Council-managed strips wilt, full of water-hungry non-natives. Succulents, everyone's favourite low-maintenance plant, creep like an invasive carpet, providing no shelter at all, barely holding the dry and cracking dirt in place. I plant what I can in places I'm not allowed, but I can't always plant food. We have a whole website and mail-in service that tells you whether your soil, the damn ground beneath your feet, is too contaminated with metals to safely grow food in. This is normal, of course. The kids play and the jacaranda trees bloom, and I wonder what little joys they simply never see.

I bite my tongue and keep my head down, keep looking. There's definitely evidence of death. Corpses, the byproducts of a suburbia red in bloody cats and cars. Lying by the side of the road, deposited by feline indifference or automobile impacts, the possums, bats, and rats come to rest. Always whole, sometimes flat. They don't rot or get eaten; just mummify, slowly, in the beating sun. Ignored by pedestrians. I make a point of taking them away and burying them. Feeding the soil. Sometimes, there are flies and maggots. Sometimes.

Our local council cares, though. Cares about the environment! About the animals! These pests might hurt our cats, so we poison them, bait them, trap them. Gas them. Hunt them down and ferret them out. A petition saved a den of people-shy foxes from being gassed, but for every indignant act of suburban outrage, there are dozens of systematic plagues against nature.

Suburbia. So damn sterile you grow to miss the cockroaches—yeah, even the ones as long as your thumb. The ones that fly. Can hardly believe it, but I miss them.

I used to dream of escaping up north to tropical Queensland, but when I visit there are always fewer clouds and more bones, more cane toads and dust. Farmers north and west don't seem to be doing much better—parched by the drought, then flooded by storms that the dead ground can't absorb. We shrug. Our supermarkets raise their prices to help farmers, but somewhere along the line forget to pass on the money. Everyone shrugs.

It goes without saying that our reefs are bleached and dying. That's not news anymore. We know this. We've accepted it. Internalised it. We don't even shrug.

I used to look with hope to the mountains and the coast, surely untouched by the creeping rot of suburban sprawl; no coddled cat vanguard, no lead in the soil, no strata rules. I looked to the same mountains and coast whose rivers are now clogged with algae and dead fish. The same mountains and coast that have burned, cloaking Sydney in hazy orange, hungrily devouring millions of acres of bushland in a single sweep. Thousands of homes, dozens of people. We shrug.

It's been more than a month, and not a single day goes by without the smell of smoke hanging thick in the air. Ash drifts from the sky. The sun rises and sets a vile, neon red, so shrouded by smoke that it's dull enough to look directly at, dull enough to be mistaken for the moon. Mood lighting, if I've ever seen it.

"Oh, it's all theoretical. It doesn't affect us! I'll believe it when I see it," they say, as the sky fills with smoke and the earth shrivels dry. "We have to think about jobs and growth. We're a nation of innovators," they say, as our livelihoods crumble and we repeat our mistakes over and over and over and—

I don't understand how we're not all furious. Look down. Look down, you fuckers. Look down, beneath your feet, under your fingernails, at the debris in your lungs, and into the silent night. Dig your hands into the dust, watch as it slips through your fingers—any damn metaphor it takes to get you to realise this country is dying around us.

Please. Look down.

These recollections were written on Gadigal land; land we have sorely mistreated. The Gadigal peoples are one of 29 clans that comprise the Eora Nation—traditional custodians of land we now call Sydney. Their sovereignty was never ceded.

Tony (they/them) spends a lot of time in the dirt, largely for therapeutic reasons. They are severely allergic to cats, and live with two cats.

The Street

The Wild Inside

Angela Penrose

We had to close up another building that day—bolt the doors shut, board over the windows, stop up the chimney and all the vents with concrete. Hank Parker came stumbling out of his house, gasping and cussing, dragging his two oldest kids by the arm while his wife huddled on the sidewalk with the three-year-old. As soon as Hank got clear, he was shaking the two kids, Lisa and Mikey, and giving them a dressing down like only a man who's devastated and angry and shocked and ashamed all at once can manage.

Thin sunlight shone down on the Parkers' neat one-story house, glinting off the clean-polished windows and making the butter-yellow siding look all warm and inviting. It showed off the perfectly cleaned and swept expanse of concrete that was the front yard, stretching flat and greyish white all around the house to where it butted up against the older sidewalk with its grainier surface and patched cracks. It was a shame to have to abandon such a nice place, but the Parkers should've known to keep watch on their kids.

I mixed fresh concrete in a barrow to one side, giving polite pretense to ignoring the verbal thunderstorm going on just a dozen steps away. From the shouting I gathered that Mikey'd been collecting leaves and flowers, pressing them into books—for a school project he said, like we didn't all know that for a lie so awkward it was embarrassing. And Lisa'd been raising some tadpoles in a jar of water. Where she'd found them I'd like to know; leaves and flowers were scarce enough in these times, much less wild creatures.

The wet concrete went scush, scush back and forth in the barrow. I scooped up a bucket of it and started up a ladder another member of the containment crew had set up for me. I was the youngest member of the team, at thirty-eight, and the hardest labor fell to me. It was the proper way to order things, even if my muscles ached for days after, each time we had to do this.

It was always the kids. Victor and I never wanted children enough to go through the hassle of a surrogate or even adoption—and having watched the play of civilized life dwindling as we all hung on as well as we could, I was just as happy to never have had that responsibility.

Keeping the kids in line—that was the trick of it.

The bam-bam-bam of hammers added percussion to the howling, snarling, whining symphony at the foot of the yard when Ynez and Chris and Peter arrived with the old, reclaimed plywood sheets and nails for the windows, and got to their task. We were running low on plywood; in another year at most, we'd have to talk about completely dismantling some of the sealed buildings for materials.

I was pouring the sixth bucket of concrete down the chimney when the shouting near the sidewalk peaked to a crescendo before cutting off, as though someone had flipped a switch on one of the stereos only those of us over twenty could remember. I looked down at the Parkers and saw that Lisa was shaking her hand at her father, her ponytail bobbing in rhythm.

"It's food!" she shouted into the aghast silence. "It's good, it's fresh, it's wonderful! It's right there to take and I don't see why we can't—"

Her mother silenced her with a hard slap across the face, then another slap at her hands sent four round, brown nuts bouncing tic-tic-tic-tic down onto the concrete.

I'd like to say I almost fell off my ladder, because it gives a dramatic beat to the story, but that'd be a lie. I stood there, my bucket dangling from one hand and the other hand locked around the top rung, because I'm not stupid.

I *was* shocked, though. I watched the nuts—hazelnuts, I think they were, although it was hard to tell from this far away—scattered across the yard, their dark, earthy brown like dirty stains on the clean cement.

Hazelnuts were from before. My mom had always bought five pounds of mixed nuts, raw in their shells, every year at Christmas. She'd kept the big bowl on the coffee table full, with nut crackers stuck into the mass and another bowl to one side for shells. We'd sit around, the adults on the couch and kids crosslegged or kneeling on the floor, talking about whatever, or listening to Christmas music, or watching TV with the sound cranked up so we could hear the dialogue around the sound of cracking shells.

Hazelnuts had always been my favorite.

I hadn't had one in years, and the packages of powdered hazelnut creamer we still found sometimes weren't the same. Victor made cookies or muffins sometimes, if the foragers came back with unspoiled flour or some kind of mix. The hazelnut powder in cookies or muffins almost reminded me of hazelnuts, more than the baked goods we could make without eggs or leavening reminded me of cookies or muffins, actually.

Real hazelnuts, though? They were dangerous.

Hank was shaking Lisa, with Mikey hanging off one of his arms. Nobody stepped in. Lisa was twelve, more than old enough to know better. Now the concrete yard would have to be scrubbed every day for a while, watched for any hint of cracks. We could lose the whole neighborhood if the wild breached the pavement.

I looked away, climbed up to the roof and poured my bucket of concrete into the chimney.

All the Parkers were screaming by then, their voices bouncing and clashing off the concrete ground, the metal siding, the glass windows, the plastered rock walls that ran all up and down the neighborhood. The discordant clash broke the orderly peace of the place, an aural mess outside to match the physical mess in their house. Their former house; the neighborhood association would have to find another place for them. Sunnyvale had always had mild weather; rain wasn't likely, so with some clean bedding, they could sleep outside for a few nights. Maybe not comfortable, but it wouldn't cause them any harm. It'd be a good lesson for the whole family, I thought. Give them a sharp experience of what an uncontrolled environment was like.

The crew and I finished our jobs some time after the dinner hour. Abe Koker was designated cook for the containment crew, in charge of making sure we got fed no matter how late we worked. The red plastic cooler sat open in one corner of his kitchen. It needed restocking; a glance told me there was only enough in it for one more meal, or maybe two if Abe stretched it.

He handed me a plate of spicy pickles stirred up with some spam crumbles and reconstituted raisins, a hunk of dense flatbread to dunk in the liquid laid across one side. I went back out front and settled on a blue plastic yard bench to eat. I'd never liked pickles before, but they kept well if they'd been made and sealed properly, and most of the vegetables we had were pickled, scooped out of dust-coated jars.

Victor came in before I finished my dinner. He sat down on the bench next to me and leaned against my shoulder.

"Damndest thing," he said.

"Yeah." I took another bite of pickled cauliflower and chewed. The fiery burn of the dried chile Abe added to most of the food he cooked covered whatever taste of spoilage might be hiding around the edges. Anyone who didn't have a cast-iron stomach had died long since; those of us left could tough out food that would've closed a restaurant down when I was a teenager.

"We should've had kids."

That stopped me in mid-chew.

"No one's said anything, but people look, you know. Carl Tulliver was chatting to me about how lonely his sister Claire has been since her husband passed. They lost all three of their kids, and he says Claire wants a baby."

I swallowed and said, "Plenty of men to give her one. Ricky Mendez has been living away from Eleanor for almost eight months now. Doesn't look like they're going to patch it up. Carl should toss Claire at Ricky, see what happens."

"It's not about specifics," Victor said, a note of impatience in his voice. "When it started, we all had other things to think about. Once things settled, we thought we had a handle on it. But it's been twenty years, nearly, and we're losing kids. Most people were ignoring it—you don't want to talk about something that hurt so many families—but you can't pretend it away anymore."

I huffed and took another bite of my pickles.

Of course I'd noticed. But we were together and I didn't feel like bringing a woman into it.

"We wouldn't have to actually be fathers," Victor said, like he'd pulled the thought out of my mind. "Just . . . you know, donate sperm. If you're really against actually having a kid. But we should contribute."

I swallowed and gave Victor a side glance. "It won't help."

"No, likely not," he admitted. "But it's not about actually fixing the problem. It's about living in the neighborhood, contributing. We shouldn't shirk this, or be miserly about it."

I knew Victor well enough to know he'd sunk his teeth into this. I avoided weeks of quiet arguments by saying, "Fine. You want to be a sperm donor, I don't mind."

He leaned over and bumped my shoulder again. "We need to fit in, be accepted," he said. I knew he was right, but I hated disruption. Our world was built around clean, orderly routine. Anything different made me wince, as viscerally as a sour note.

I finished eating, then Victor and I walked over to the school for band practice.

Seventeen of us in the neighborhood had played instruments before, and managed to keep them working and maintained through the upheaval. We didn't have enough power for the constant electronic entertainment I'd wallowed in as a kid, even when we could find a music player. If we wanted music, we had to make it the old fashioned way. I didn't really mind. I'd been a band geek all through school, but finding a group of adults to play with was tough unless you wanted to commit to a city orchestra, or Have A Band and hustle for gigs. There never seemed to be enough time for that back when I was a newbie electrical engineer with a busy life ahead of me.

Fourteen of us made it to the band room that evening. Bodies warmed the room a little, and it'd heat up more when the audience arrived. The matted carpet was a dirty grey-tan under our feet, but it was clean; we scrubbed it with detergent and brooms every other week. The folding metal chairs fought back against our butts, it seemed, but standing was worse. The candle smoke perfumed the air with a hodge-podge of paraffin and ancient perfume—vanilla and rose and jasmine and pine and pumpkin. Candles lasted if you didn't burn them, and folks were usually sparing of them. Everyone brought candles on band night, though.

We had a great session. We messed around at first, practicing and trading riffs, trying new things. After the first hour, other people filtered in, to stand or sit around the periphery and listen. We moved into playing actual songs then, and went through a couple of sets, with a water break in the middle.

Music lets me focus on something else. It's something that's real, but not. You can't see it or touch it, it's just vibrations in the air. If you do it right, its effect is way beyond what "vibrations in the air" should be, but there you go. You can follow it into its own world. It's transformative, and evocative. You can work it the way you'd ration your water, or you can play with it the way we used to mess with video games—vitally important and completely irrelevant, both, depending on what you put into it and what you wanted to take from it.

I needed to play that night. By the light of the hoarded candle ends, I threw myself into my trumpet and let myself just have fun. Victor could jam with his flute, and the two of us swirled around each other, teasing and challenging and practically having aural sex right there in the air above everyone. The other band members followed along and the fun multiplied. The clapping and tapping and singing of the people in our audience took it to another exponent, and we all rocked, defying the wild with our celebration of perfectly timed and ordered notes vibrating through the air.

Afterward, Victor and I volunteered to clean up. Everyone else left while we took our time cleaning our instruments and putting them away. Victor used a long-handled broom to scrub a few smudges of soot that candle smoke had left on the white ceiling. I polished a window that'd had three people sitting on its sill for two hours, making the glass shine clear.

We didn't hurry. I'll admit we paused here and there for some making out, because we might've been approaching middle age but we weren't dead.

By the time we left, most folks in the neighborhood were in bed. There wasn't much you could do in the dark—talking, singing and sex were pretty much it. So when I heard a light, rhythmic crunching over in the dark where the fence was, on the far side of the school playground, I put a hand on Victor's arm.

Crunch-crunch-crunch, barely audible footsteps in the gravel, low but clear in the crisp night air.

I exchanged a look with Victor and we swerved in the direction of the playground fence, walking as lightly as we could. I steered us toward the deepest darkness; it wasn't a direct line to the source of the sounds, but I was pretty sure I knew what was out there, and I didn't want to have to break into an all-out run any sooner than I had to.

We followed whoever it was, timing our footsteps to match theirs, away from the school and between a pair of houses that'd been abandoned years ago, all the paved ground between the buildings open—we'd scavenged every backyard fence within a dozen miles years ago.

We crossed a street, passed through yards of dirty pavement that no one had tended in weeks. One patio was a mass of cracks and fissures, with twisted rows of plants growing through, like crazy hedges a finger-length tall. The houses themselves were sealed with plywood and bolts and concrete, holding off the invasion of the wild, but we didn't have enough people to keep every bit of it clean and orderly, and this far away from the neighborhood there were cracks in our defenses.

I felt prickling fear run up and down my back as we walked through the living chaos. Anything could be there in the lightless spaces under the eaves and beside the chimney, or the deep shadows between houses where even the moonlight couldn't penetrate.

Across pitted asphalt and badly patched cement, following the footsteps. The nearest inhabited houses were blocks away now, and every minute or so I heard a shred of voice blow past on the wind. I couldn't distinguish words, nor recognize the voices, but I knew who was ahead of us.

Victor and I had longer legs, and eventually we could see the moving shadows ahead of us—a taller figure with a ponytail, a shorter figure carrying a long stick. In the twists and turns between buildings, I saw that both shapes had the humpbacked silhouette that meant backpacks.

Running away seemed like an extreme reaction for the Parker kids. Their parents had been mad, sure, but how did two kids expect to be able to survive on their own?

Dumb question—they were kids. Ten- and twelve-year-olds might be a lot more capable now than when I was that age, out of necessity, but they were still kids, which meant they didn't think things through. Didn't have all the info, didn't have the judgement, and were likely to just assume things would work out the way they wanted.

The wind brought shreds of stressed voices back to us, along with a quickened patter of sneakers on concrete. I expected them to swerve off the street and duck between houses again, try to lose us, but they just tore straight down the block, heading in the direction of the old mall.

We might have longer legs, but Victor and I were a lot older, and kids've always had energy to spare. Their small shapes grew closer at first, gaining detail in the moonlight, but half a minute later they were gaining again, and I could hear Victor gasping for breath next to me.

I pushed on, not willing to lose two more kids for the neighborhood.

The street we ran down spread wide enough for six cars, and up ahead I saw an intersection like a city plaza. The asphalt river ran between islands of concrete, mountains of stucco and steel and siding rising up, square-edged, on either side. There was an older shopping center—a few short blocks of city streets lined with shops—just this side of the larger and slightly newer mall. Rustic and twisty, designed to make it seem bigger than it was, Lisa and Mikey likely thought they could lose us there. They might be right.

The bigger shadow, Lisa, put on some extra speed and dragged her brother into the shopping center. They vanished around a corner; Victor and I got there as fast as we could, but there was no one in sight when we rounded it.

"Keep looking," I hissed, trying to be quiet while panting hard. "We've got to find them." I waved him on down the main drag while I took the first turn to the right, between what'd been a drug store and a shoe store.

I remembered working with the containment team, sealing up the shops right behind the foragers who were hauling everything out, everything that might conceivably be useful some day.

The decorative wooden pillars that held up the clay tile roof extending out to the edge of the sidewalk from the rows of stores had been engulfed in ivy. Without regular maintenance, wood cracks and weathers. We'd torn it all off when we sealed the structures, but ivy is fierce and voracious, and without constant battle it'll always regroup and surge forward into any territory it can claim. The ivy on the shop walls, under the awning, got little sun; straggly and thin, it left only a bare garrison to hold its captured walls. I stayed in the street, well away from the wild greenery, but that just meant I could see where it covered the pillars and the roof, dark and thick, mounds of the stuff.

I felt my skin crawl just being near it. Any greenery was creepy, but ivy? It was made to strangle, and it could have anything lurking in it, hidden by the leaves. Bugs? Even wild animals? What were the kids thinking, choosing such a place to hide?

Maybe they thought we wouldn't follow them?

I was creeped out, yes, but it made me that much more determined to find the kids and get them away.

I stopped and listened. I heard Victor calling. That'd just let Lisa and Mikey know where he was so they could avoid him. Once he was done with his shouting, though, I heard the pet-pet-pet sound of running sneakers on asphalt coming from the south, in the direction of the mall.

That made no sense. The older shopping center was infested with the wild, but kids at that in-between age were often less wary than they should be. I'd expected them to try to lose us here and then dash off to one of the surrounding neighborhoods, either east or west. The mall, though, was surrounded by open expanses of asphalt. Its old parking lots were easily patched, so nothing grew there. They provided no cover. I rushed on south, expecting to see Lisa and Mikey as soon as I got clear of the shopping center.

Sure enough, they were just dashing around the leftmost corner of an old anchor store, dark shadows against the dirty beige stucco, stark in the moonlight.

Footsteps pounded behind me and a glance over my shoulder showed that Victor had figured out where the action was. He was still a block and a half behind, though; the night air carried sound so well I'd hoped he was closer.

I rounded the corner, pivoting with one hand on a lamp-post that creaked and left my palm gritty. There, Lisa and Mikey hunched near where the store entrance used to be.

I thought they'd given up—run out of juice, maybe—and I slowed to a fast walk, sucking oxygen in heaving gasps. Then I heard a sharp creak and Lisa vanished. I squinted into the darkness, trying to see whether she'd just moved into a deeper shadow, or maybe crouched down behind her brother, but I couldn't see any sign of her. Then Mikey ducked down and he was gone too.

Inside. They'd gone inside.

I shouted for Victor and ran up to where the kids had disappeared. The whole side of the building was dark, but when I got within arm's reach I could see that the plywood nailed over the wide doorway had been pried up. The very bottom looked like it hadn't been nailed at all, and when I tugged on the lower corner, it pulled a few inches away from the wall. There still wasn't enough clearance for me to get through; the kids would've barely fit.

I started pulling hard, and heard more nails loosening and the wood giving way—crack, crack, crack.

Victor came pounding up, gasping for breath. "What —whadyou—doing?!"

"The kids went inside. We have to get them out. Help me."

"Crazy!" Victor huffed, but he got his hands on the edge of the plywood and yanked with me.

It was probably less than half a minute before the board gave a final snap and hinged outward, leaving a gaping hole.

Light streamed out. The air that puffed out of the gap was humid and slightly warm. The floor just inside rose up higher than the threshold of the old door, thick with dirt and loam, leaves and twigs, and in the light that seemed to be glowing softly from every direction at once in there, I could see little things with lots of legs moving around, over the twigs and under the leaves.

I could feel adrenaline pumping through my veins and sweat dampening the back of my neck. This was wild, the wild inside, the wild we fought to keep out of our houses with constant maintenance, watchful vigilance, scraping away every blade of grass and sprout and leaf. This...this was lost.

I swallowed hard and crawled inside, scrambling to my feet as soon as I could, hopefully before any of the crawling bug-things got on me.

Inside, I looked around and almost lost my balance.

The door was still behind me—I looked around and checked and saw Victor's head poking in—but it was just a hole in what looked like a cliff face. The ground I was standing on sloped sharply down starting just a step or two away from the hole. Huge trees and dense bushes grew all around, softening the slope and whatever gouges and gaps there might be in the...well, the cliff face.

In front of me the land was gashed by a narrow canyon, running farther than I could see right and left. It was only about a hundred or so feet across, but there was no way over, no bridge, nothing at all that looked constructed. Everything I could see was leaves and fronds and blossoms and grass. A bird went swooping out of an overhanging tree and down into the canyon where it vanished beyond the lip. Something with grey fur skittered up the trunk of a tree farther on.

"Do you see the kids?" asked Victor, his voice hushed. "Any sign?"

Right, the kids. I looked down, figuring I could pick up their tracks with the ground all soft. Sure enough, there were two sets of impressions. They weren't sharp like on dusty concrete, but a long, ovalish depression in the leaf litter that repeated alternately right, left, right. The tracks headed off to the left, around an outcropping that bulged out from the cliff where the door was, then vanished. I took a couple of steps, following the tracks, moving slow and deliberate. The outcrop was patchy with feathered lichens and the occasional tuft of velvet moss. A grey bulge suddenly scuttled away—it was a lizard, but I'd thought it was a piece of the rock, and when it moved I jumped.

Bright green birds with scarlet heads launched themselves up off the rock over my head and dove down at me, the whole flock of them. I hollered in fright and ducked down with my arms curled over my head. From my crouching position I could see a fuzzy worm of some kind crawling up my pants leg with a sickening, undulating sort of movement. I dashed it off with my hand, then scrubbed my hand on the fabric of my pants.

A snake appeared, dangling from a branch, its forked tongue quavering at me, like it was tasting the air, trying to taste me. A shivering wave of terror gripped me and I turned and fled back to the door.

Shoving Victor aside, I crawled through, back out to the clean world where nothing wanted to crawl on my body.

"What is it? What'd you see?" Victor was back on his feet, poised to either run or grapple something.

"It's lost," I said, shoving the plywood back into place over the door. It wouldn't be enough, of course. "It's completely wild. We need to seal it, and not just plywood."

"But the kids—?"

"They're lost," I said. I felt like I had a rock in my throat, or that snake, something slithering down and down and down into my belly so I couldn't swallow, couldn't breathe. I leaned against the broken plywood sheet and tried to catch my breath, slow my slamming heart. "I'll stay. Go get the team—wood, bolts, concrete, everything. We need to seal this tonight."

Victor nodded, his face all grim, down-turned angles. He gave me a hard hug, then trotted off.

I stood there with my back against the door. I hoped the kids would come out, that Lisa or Mikey or both would come to their senses and come home with us. I hoped, but I knew it wouldn't happen. It never did. Still, I waited there, hands spread to feel for knocking, listening for voices, footsteps. I waited and listened until Victor came back with the others, and we started pouring concrete.

Angela Penrose lives in Seattle with her husband, seven computers, and about ten thousand books. She writes in several genres, but SFF is her first love. She majored in history at college, but racked up hundreds of units taking whatever looked interesting. This delayed graduation to a ridiculous degree, but (along with obsessive reading) gave her a broad store of weirdly diverse information that comes in wonderfully handy to a writer. She's had stories published in *Loosed Upon the World*, *Fiction River*, and *Alien Artifacts*. Find more of Angie's fiction at http://angelapenrosewriter.blogspot.com/p/blog-page.html.

you said, "they're making the ground soft"

Christy Jones

maybe ground is meant to ripple
and sag like skin showing

her age. the wisdom
of roots aching to surface

maybe we're meant to stumble
and break blades made for vain

manicuring to steep amazement
in unpredictable growth

you downed nana cottonwood onto
teenaged limbs, too young

to hold weighted life, a shock
of white, stripped bark and sodden

leaves. the birds stand on it all, ever
resilient, flexible. these will be new

nests. there is no pride here, only
adjustment, as there always is

when the flightless impose
their ground on the sky

Christy Jones is a Minnesotan poet, singer, actress, and playwright. She completed her MFA in Creative Writing from Lindenwood University, and has works published or forthcoming in *The Collidescope*, *Eunoia Review*, *Crêpe & Penn*, *Quatrain.Fish*, *Crux Literary Journal*, and *Scarlet Leaf Review*. She'll defend the honor of musical theater, linguistics, empathy, and Duck, Duck, Gray Duck to her dying day.

On the Destruction and Restoration of Habitats

Priya Chand

The forest preserve district wants me to cut down trees. With a saw in one hand and loppers in the other, I oblige.

As a child I got my destructive tendencies out in videogames and martial arts. Beating all of my friends at Street Fighter—and gloating about it—was fine. Plucking flowers was not. Even the ubiquitous dandelions like tiny weak suns in the lawn grass were meant to be seen, and only pulled once transmogrified to puff-ball form, wanting dispersal.

At the beginning of May this year, I ripped those vivid yellow heads off every single dandelion in my parents' yard, and then when more had bloomed the next day I did it again.

After I'd dumped the pile of them into the trash, I went to the little patch of trees across the street. The grass here was sparse, a bloom of mushrooms welled from the drying mud. I squatted down and took a minute to admire a single violet plant. Heart shaped leaves framed purple flowers. The flowers are easily recognized even when they aren't purple. The white ones are indigo-streaked to lead in the pollinators, but my favorite, for the irony and more, are the yellow violets. They are bright, though nestled close to the ground, and not as shiny as the five-petaled swamp buttercups that, as their name suggests, thrive alongside Illinois' transient and permanent wetlands.

All these native plants and more—the mayapples, trillium, spring beauties, Dutchman's breeches, woodland phlox; and those are only the current season's more common flowers—evolved to thrive in specific conditions. Varying degrees of sunlight and wetness will even introduce variations within a species. The most vivid specimen of spring beauties I have ever seen, with shocking pink anthers that would put Barbie to shame, was about a minute after my sneaker filled with muddy water because of snowmelt on the unpaved trail. But I've also seen them growing in flocks in the grass, out in full sun, the characteristic pink lines on their petals faded to a more solemn hue.

But none of these thrive in the presence of invaders.

Garlic mustard pops up in the spring, leaves somewhat reminiscent of violets', with little clusters of four-petaled white flowers. The roots smell like garlic, which is how it got the name, and it generates chemicals that kill its neighbors. When I see it, I rip it out—it's not as persistent as dandelion. My family finds this very annoying when we're out walking, but how can I squander the privilege of this knowledge, this access to the woodlands?

Before I found the local forest preserve, I joined whatever volunteer opportunities in habitat restoration came my way. Some of these included local youth. They came from various backgrounds, but the important thing was they were interested in the program, even when their destructive tendencies were less delicate than mine.

One year we were supposed to take a group of middle schoolers to plant trees in an impoverished neighborhood, which had its nature overwritten in concrete and scraggly grass. Of course, a group of middle schoolers and a few adults can't dig all the holes needed for oak saplings. So the plan was—if I remember correctly— for the community service workers to dig the holes, leaving the saplings with their root balls for the kids to plop in and cover with dirt. Satisfying, right?

When we got there, there had been a mix up. The holes were not dug and there were only a few saplings.

Unable to do anything, the leader improvised a plan: cleanup. We would walk around picking up trash. Dime bags the kids didn't understand (and we didn't explain), thankfully—that time—no condom wrappers, and the litter of any place, even those where everyone has a reusable tote bag. Organic bars come in the same metallic wraps as their cheaper cousins.

We came to a tree, a slim thing caged by its surroundings, spreading thin leaves despite the mound of cigarette butts around it.

I'll never forget the look on the kids' faces. Why would people make such a mess, right there? It was a learning opportunity, to see the bar across the street and recall the order banning indoors smoking. Unintended consequences. Easily changed by being mindful of one's own behavior. They cared, and I hope still care. I hope that when they are adults out on field trips, they don't have to try to hide, at the end of an otherwise excellent kayak up our manmade lagoons, surrounded by squawking birds and shy turtles and the sinuous movement of water gliders, in the middle of the clear summer sky a blot of a cormorant dangling from a tree by the fishing line stuck in its throat.

My pathetic diversion didn't work, because these were curious kids with functioning eyes and senses attuned after a solid hour looking for animals. But it didn't stop them from continuing to participate in learning about and restoring nature. Not everything we do outside has to be a conquest.

Buckthorn, like garlic mustard, is allelopathic. It releases chemicals that kill its neighbors. There was one morning where, I swear, the second the last virulent orange trunk hit the earth, the frogs struck up their song, sunlight warming the newly cleared space. Thankfully buckthorn doesn't grow amid standing water, but it had been close to the edge.

While it's incredibly satisfying to yell "Timber!" as the creaking turns into a crash, the buckthorn isn't actually dead. The thing about invasives is they're not immigrants or foreigners, they are colonists. Killing their competitors is only the first step: they have to be able to grow and reproduce, too. As long as its roots are alive, buckthorn has the opportunity to send up whippy shoots en masse. When these have the opportunity to grow, they create a whole tangle that's hard to cut down, tangled trunks and branches, and of course the thorns they're named after.

The only solution is to destroy even the roots, by painting a herbicide onto the trunks that will leach through.

You may have heard of this one.

It's called glyphosate.

When it's not damaging farm workers and bees, glyphosate is saving habitats by killing off the invasives that destroy our habitats, the rare plants and animals which adapted to their niches over the course of millennia, only to be derailed by a succession of introductions both intentional and otherwise.

Paying extra for organic produce, living in a place with enough volunteers and staff to maintain the woods that release crisp, fresh air from their rich green leaves, the carpet of moss and grass and flowers underfoot attracting birds that sit up in the branches and trill away, with no consideration for an amateur photographer—it is easy to not understand why things like glyphosate still exist, are still used.

But until there is another solution, our options are limited. We cannot go back in time to save that biodiversity before it ever became threatened, before the pale furl of a blue flag iris beneath its stiff proud leaves became a rare event. We must move forward.

Until there are better options, I will be in the forest, sawing down trees and pulling weeds, with the other regular volunteers and student groups that still, in the middle of a million other assaults on nature, take the time to try and heal this piece.

You're invited.

Priya Chand majored in biology, with serious plans to never venture into fieldwork. She is now a volunteer steward with the local forest preserve, assisting primarily with the removal of invasive species. Her resume lists this as being a "hobbyist lumberjack." Find her online at priyachandwrites.wordpress.com.

Owl Prowl

Maya Chhabra

My fiancée's aunt takes us to look for owls.
We wear ice cleats. New family, new ways,
but I'm an indoor cat (cats are another thing
I've had to learn). I am new at this, new
as the ring on my finger, but my love
puts on earmuffs and glows in the full moon.
I pull up my hood. We stand in a circle
and strain for owl calls. *Who-cooks-for-you?*
Who-cooks-for-you? my new aunt calls, but no,
no owls come. Stillness. I hear the highway
and people shifting their weight, the ice cracking.
I'm an indoor cat, bundled up, impatient, but
I won't ruin this pristine moment, not with
my love standing eager in the pale light.
I brace myself for a long and frozen watch.

But the wind dies down and the quiet trees
shield us as best they can. In my borrowed boots,
I stamp up and downhill, crushing crystals,
making the path safe. The night dilates our eyes.
as we wait in the cold, in the bright forest hush,
standing next to each other, facing out.
No owls come. And after all, it's not so terrible.

Maya Chhabra is the author of the novel *Stranger on the Home Front* and various pieces of short fiction, poetry, and translation. Her work has appeared in *Strange Horizons*, *Daily Science Fiction*, and *Cast of Wonders*, and been nominated for the Rhysling Award. She lives in Brooklyn with her partner.

Riverine

Danielle Jorgenson Murray

The house was wide open, all the windows lit with yellow light of a warmer shade than he'd ever seen in the city, and the table was laid for one. That was the way my father always told it. It was a strange tale to tell a child at bedtime, but I loved him to recount every detail—each dish set out for him, every floral pattern on every serving spoon. I marvelled at the exacting strength of his memory. As children we know our parents cannot lie to us whom they love so well.

He told me with relish as great as his story-self's hunger about the owner of the house. A man, sometimes, with a heron's neck or an otter's smile or the glittering eyes of a damselfly, the rippling sheen of flowing water on his skin. The river man. My father made him sound beautiful, a creature of unknowable thoughts and unimaginable power, so when he got to the part where he promised this unearthly man to me in marriage, my heart fluttered with desire and excitement, my eyes wide. That was the part I made him repeat the most.

Walking out of the city, I am no longer sure whether I ever believed it was true.

The road to the river becomes greener than all the other roads, like a tributary bleeding slyly up into the city. At first you notice only skinny grass verges mowed to stubble, yellow as hay, and then low-growing daisies begin to gleam through, vying for your eye with litter thrown from car windows. You imagine the council men in fluorescent jackets wandering away with their strimmers, bemused, one by one, as the river man turns them away.

Under the bridge you must cross to get there flows an endless stream of cars instead of water. I hike up my wedding clothes to climb the steps. I'll just be a flash of white to the people in their cars, a curiosity they'll forget in a minute.

By the time I get to the river the vegetation is wild, a tangle of plaited sticks and old leaves, scrapes and burrows among the roots. My gloves and damp skirt keep catching my eye, winking like sunlight on snow. He was promised to me like a gift, but I'm the one who's wrapped up and presentable.

I'm excited for this. But maybe part of all excitement is terror.

The grassy track leads to a garden without walls and a house I know from a lifetime of stories.

There's a table in the garden barely visible under dishes I've spent hours imagining. The only difference between the real table and the story one is that this one is set for two, and my husband is seated there, watching me come into his home with dark animal eyes.

I don't know how to greet a husband. I don't know his name, if he has one. I don't know if he knows mine. He doesn't look happy to see me. He doesn't look glad to be mine.

"Sit," he says, and I almost burst into tears, certain I've been tricked somehow. I manage to sit beside him in the wooden chair, perhaps the same chair in which my father sat when he met my husband. The thought calms my shivering a little. "Eat," says my husband. "This is your home now."

I have friends with married sisters, who all say a bride can never eat on her wedding day. I thought it was some kind of rule, but now I understand. This whole feast laid out before me, and me in my clean white wedding clothes. It feels like a setup for a photograph, imitation food like the imitation diploma you get photographed with when you graduate so you don't smudge and crease your real one with your anxious, sweaty hands. A bride doesn't eat on her wedding day. You wouldn't remember it anyway.

"What would you like?" asks my husband.

I think I'd like not to be married.

"What is there?" I ask, at a loss. I'm almost too scared to look at the dishes—pies and soups and salads.

He points, my husband, and his fingers are feathered in the black and brown bars and scallops of a female mallard's plumage. He names every ingredient, many of which I have only heard of from my father's story, and I choose almost at random. He serves me with a wide wooden spoon. Everything is wood but the knife blades, which are all mismatched in their settings. I've never seen so much wood in one place. No plastic or silicon or china, and what metal there is shines strangely, rough-textured.

This is a gift. My father arranged this for me because he loves me and wants me to be happy, and the river man is better than any of the city boys I've ever known.

And there's that feeling again, of being tricked, because if the river man is a gift, then you'd expect I could refuse it, decline it, send it back. But I don't think I can. And what's a gift you can't refuse?

Married life is not what I expected it to be. The river man is some-how never around and everywhere all at once. We eat together, always, and though the table is laden with a wide variety of dishes for me—damp, cool salads, roasted goose legs, roots and berries and dried fruits I don't recognise—he eats only a little, and different every day. His head might be a cormorant's, and then he'll skewer fish on his beak and swallow them down whole, or he might have a fish's bony plated face, in which case he will immerse his head in a bowl of water and nibble at weeds. Once it was something mon-strously insectile. I feared a mosquito's head on my husband's body and a meal of blood at our table, but he ate nothing at all. Some short-lived flying creature whose adult form has no mouth, its body designed only to breed.

I sat awake in my room that night, wondering if he would be overcome by that other frenetic appetite, but I slept alone (when I slept at last), as I always did.

He speaks little. Sometimes out of necessity, when he is beaked or billed, when his throat has no vocal chords or his fangs get in the way. But even when his head is the head of a man or woman he keeps his words to himself, speaking only to ask me the barest question or tell me what I may or may not do.

"You can roam as you will," he tells me at breakfast as I'm picking eggshell off the table. "You can swim in any water except the place beneath the alders."

I know that alders are a kind of tree but not where they grow. "Why?" I ask, of all the questions.

"It doesn't matter to you why," he says.

How can he know without asking me? This is my home too.

"You're my husband," I find myself saying, the lightest emphasis on the possessive.

He quiets me with a look. Today his eyes are amber, the pupils round and sharply delineated. I can't recognise them. I think he might speak, but he doesn't. He's angry, though his eyes only continue to bore into me and his body ripples like an endless flow of water, a river in vaguely human shape. There is no body language there to read. But I know.

Because I questioned him? Because I won't be denied my freedom? I'm beginning to understand the kind of life I've fallen into. There are places I may not go, and this outrages me in a way I can barely give shape to in my own mind.

I discover the little marsh by swimming.

I associate swimming with the smell of chlorine, blue-tiled pools, the feel of cold lycra. There's none of that here. Just me and water.

No; me and water and mud and stones, and soft caressing weed like hair, and floating leaves and skimming insects and tiny darts of fish. There are waterbirds that dive beneath me and bob around my shoulders and kick water in my face when they decide they've had enough of me. Sometimes when something touches me I pull away, like a leg under a restaurant table opposite a stranger. Sometimes I reach out with open fingers and touch back, curious, unfurling.

I enjoy being changeable like this. I can be difficult and fickle here in my own private place, in a way I have never been able to do anywhere else.

The city was crammed with other people. You could see them through windows, or walking down the street. You could hear them through the walls. You could smell where they had been in perfume and sweat. And you knew that in all of these ways your own life was laid bare to anyone who wanted to see it.

I can feel the difference in the water as it gets more intimate with the land, the grittiness of it, a murkiness I can feel as well as see. I might be swimming in an entirely different river. The trees are different too, their skeletons spindlier. Woody brown things drift on the surface like petrified flowers. I begin to wade waist-deep, moving slow and dreamlike. The water has left brown tidemarks and stains on my collarbone and arms.

I've never seen another footprint by the river. I've never heard distant voices beyond the trees. No voice but my husband's. No print but his mutable feet. The birdsong is mine and the current is mine. The thorns on the branches and the shells in the pebbles and the hard, sticky buds waiting for spring.

I don't think this is how rivers are supposed to run, so cold and clear over their stones and then spread out luxuriously around a corner into this tree-studded water meadow. All of this is his wedding gift to me, and I think, capriciously, that maybe this could be enough for me to stay and be happy.

Something inside me that I've never known was empty is suddenly full. I wade past strange small flowers and wonder have I been so starved of privacy? Have I only wanted to be reassured that there are still places that we haven't touched? The shape of this new fullness is too complicated; I can't get it all in my head at once.

There are marks in some of the tree trunks, scrapes and splinters like they were gouged by teeth. Birds flicker at the edges of my vision. Flies skim silently over the water, making ripples like raindrops. Nothing's ever quiet like this without a reason.

Something splashes and I pause my own splashing. A dark, low shape glides along the blurry bank. The teeth marks on the trees. Beavers. But—

There's a sound that I wasn't expecting and can't parse. It might be vegetable or animal, tearing or growling. Something else moves among the trees. It looks black and heavy, strong. A boar when it turns in just the right way. It looks like it would sink faster than a stone. It snuffles closer so I stand taller and try to project my energy outwards—*Go away. Don't bother me.* It takes no interest in me.

The next visitors are dogs, and they are very interested.

I, slightly disappointed, resign myself to the truth: that I've waded naked into an ordinary scrap of the woodland the city has allowed to remain, where people can walk and shade out the buildings from their view for an hour or two, and pretend they can't hear cars anymore. I glance upwards, looking for aeroplane trails.

The dogs come closer, trailing no leads and wearing no collars, followed by no echoing voice calling their human-given names.

I move backwards and they watch me from the bank, mud up their legs, as though asking if I've realised what they are. One of them lowers its head, then another, and a couple begin to pace as if weighing up the prospect of me. How could I have mistaken them for anything but wolves? I back away, slow and clumsy, clouds of silt caressing my thighs, some strand of weed tightening across my Achilles tendon and snapping in slow, soft motion. The wolves follow me down at a comfortable pace.

I need to get back to the deep running water where I can swim, though I think of my legs, long and trailing like a fishing line off the back of a boat, waiting to be snapped. I must be getting close to home now. I turn my back on the wolves to see the same trees lining this slow, wide flow, with no sign at all of the riverbank I know. There's a splash, then another, as my mind's eye recreates perfectly the wolves coming into the water one by one. I rock and sway and no matter how hard I try I can't move fast enough against this weight of water. The quiet is shattered with splashing now, the wolves' and mine. My feet get caught in plants and mud, and the little sharp stones find the soft parts of my soles. I lose my footing, fall and keep on falling. I don't land; my outstretched arms never touch the silty river bottom. I am being carried by the water in an infinite forward motion. Under now, spluttering uselessly.

I break the surface; my lungs take in air and my eyes take in sky in one quick deep gasp before I right myself again. The current is with me, bearing me up and away.

My husband stands on the bank, his eyes on me, and just as I recognise him he bends over and becomes wolf, and when the pack trots up the bank and away, pausing to shake water from their coats, he goes with them.

I stretch my legs to stand and wade indignantly against the current to demand to know whose side he is on, but the river ushers me away. I look over my shoulder to see only the cold waters I'm used to. Around the bend will be our house. I look back to him but the marsh is gone too, swallowed up by clean blue-grey shades of rock and water.

"I told you not to swim under the alders," says my husband that night.

I don't waste time being surprised. "I didn't know those were alders," I say. "I didn't know what alders looked like."

"You could have asked," says my husband, his eyes like black beads or dark pools. "I would have told you."

For once my thoughts and words are in harmony. "You can't just give me all the freedom in the world with one arbitrary restriction."

"It was not arbitrary," he says.

"Then you should have told me the reason why when I asked you! I would have understood if there was a reason—"

"There was a reason."

"—and I would have been more careful!" My voice has got so loud. If he'd answered when I'd asked then I might well have asked what alders look like and where they grow. There's no way to prove I wouldn't have.

"Why would your behaviour change?" he asks. "The reason is the same whether you know it or not."

My feelings are all tangling up inside me now. "If you'd only told me there were wolves—"

"The wolves were not the reason," he interrupts, because nothing can be easy with him.

And he went with *them*, not with me. He ran with them, and he left me alone in the mud and cold water. The image of him taking to four legs, waving his tail, sears itself in my mind so I know I'll see it faint over every other thought I'll ever have, and this childish jealousy crackling beneath it. The words refuse to form. "What was the reason, then?" I force myself to ask.

"The reason does not concern you," says my husband.

The dam in my mind holds for now. I don't shout at him the way I want to. I can only look at him and dare him to read all of these unspoken thoughts in my face if he can. Then even looking is too much, and I have to turn away.

"That place was not for you," he says. I think I can tell the colours of some of his moods. I think he is asking a question of me. I think he is saying different things every time he repeats this thought. He wants me to understand or explain. Well, I can't.

"I don't understand," I say flatly.

"Not everywhere is for everyone," he says. "No one can have everywhere."

"Except you." The words slip past the dam.

"No." His voice is gentle. I look back up at him, as though I'm looking for something and have almost found it. It isn't there, whatever it is, in his face. His whiskers twitch a little in the breeze and that's all. "You know what I am."

What is it that I think I know? That he's the river man. That he can't leave this place any more than I can fly out of my own body. "You know what *I* am."

Whatever he expects of me is unfair.

"You won't cause trouble here," he says. It isn't even an order, just a fact.

"I wouldn't have done anything," I retort, stung. What does he think I am? What kind of vandal? He's *mine*, and he ran with wolves rather than say a word to me, and I'll never forget that.

"You wouldn't have known if you did."

"Did I?"

He says nothing.

"If you'd *told* me," I begin, but he can't bear to have it out again, and says, "Your kind can't be trusted with knowing what isn't your business. You haven't changed."

I swear he doesn't raise his voice, but it gets louder anyway. The wind, the crash of water, the sound of stones, all of this is behind his words but his voice doesn't change at all.

Though I know we are of different kinds his words set a fire behind my eyes. "What does my *kind* have to do with anything? I'm your wife, and if you're only going to play games with me then why agree to my father's terms in the first place?"

He doesn't grow but he is larger all the same; towering, broad and with a kind of dynamic force even though he stands still.

I rise up from my seat, angry but careful. It feels obscene to upset this table, to scuff the chair legs against the ground and make the dishes clatter.

I run into the house, leaving the food to cool on the table. Leave it for the flies, the voles, the riverside foxes. I slam the door of my room and the presence of the walls is a weighted blanket of comfort. I draw the curtains to block out the view of the river, of my husband.

I haven't thought about my father's stories for a long time. I'm staring at the door, and it surprises me how safe I feel. He's never come in here, not once. The table where we eat is outside. The river is outside so he is outside. Not everywhere is for everyone, he said.

I open the door onto the quiet landing, and leave it open all night.

For the next few days I stay inside, almost daring him to come in.

The quiet inside the house is too quiet. There are no other people nestled wall to wall and ceiling to floor with me, their lives spilling out into mine. I never thought I'd miss that constant sound.

I sit at our table in the evening, comfortably cool, the silence pressing in on me but at the same time unbreakable. It would only take a word, but I can't, until my husband appears through the bushes, as though he's come out from the river itself, stepped up onto those scattered rocks that stand up, green-bearded, from the water, and onto the hard-packed mud. I don't know if he's surprised to see me here waiting for him. He turns his head to look at me out of a cormorant eye, his beak daggerlike.

"I'd like to visit my family," I say. It's not really a question but it feels like one. How much of the story was ever true?

My husband's eyes seem to flicker as he blinks. He comes to the table the long way around, away from me. I watch him walk openly, the way the light plays on the tight, sleek feathers down his neck, the way the leaves and slim vines around his arms quiver stiffly with his movements. Eventually he sits beside me, smelling of fish and sap. He won't speak tonight. "I'll go tomorrow," I say. "I don't know when I'll come back, but I will."

His wordlessness softens my heart towards him. It's easy to take for a kind of powerlessness.

I find myself reaching out, and I touch him timidly on the arm, brushing a green leaf. He doesn't move, his eye still fixed on me and his beak pointed away. Emboldened by the freedom waiting for me tomorrow, I reach higher, where his shoulder and neck meet and the feathers grow, and touch them so softly I barely disturb them. They give under my fingers, though they look as though they should be sharp.

His feathers lift all at once in a shudder, and I pull my hand away. They settle again into the sleek unbroken surface, and he doesn't move, only continues to watch me. I don't know if I'm allowed to touch him again, or if he wants me to. Either way, my courage has finally run out, and I look away.

I've been missing my old life so badly, but once I'm out of my riverside haven and back on the road, I feel like I've come to a place I've never been before. I've never noticed cars were so loud. Above me the sky is streaked with white furred vapour trails and the planes move too straight and steady, glint in the sun. They're loud too, hissing and roaring above to drown out my own train of thought.

The ground gives way to tarmac, paving stones, concrete that has dried like dough on a kneading board.

I cross the bridge that will take me back home, my husband all but gone from my mind. I rise above the oppressive smell the cars leave in their wake, strong and somehow new to me though I must have been reared in it. It's only something familiar seen from a new angle, but it's all the stranger for that.

The further into the city I get, the easier my steps become. My feet still know the way. I could walk blindfolded and still get home. I'd have a harder time not ending up at my doorstep.

Some of the shops on the row are new, but I can't remember what they used to be. The sign of what might have been an old launderette has been taken off to reveal letters bleached into the bricks, a family butcher's which hasn't been there since before I was born.

I wonder what day it is. What year. How old am I, or am I a ghost in a muddle of eras?

The door that used to be mine buzzes and opens.

As soon as I see my father's face it's as though I've never been away.

"Ey, flower," he says, "you come inside."

The matter of what story I'll tell him is half-solved because he's already chosen what he wants to believe. The kettle is already beginning to hiss before the door closes.

"It's normal to fight," he says. "Especially in your circumstances, with no time to get used to each other. I should have—"

"We didn't fight," I interrupt, and it doesn't feel like a lie even though it is, and my cheeks are hot and red. "I just thought I'd visit home. It's been a long time."

He doesn't quite believe me, but he approves of my direction nonetheless. I suppose it shows willing. "And he knows you're here, does he?" His voice is all sympathy, but I wouldn't blame him for being wary of the river man's wrath.

"Of course he knows," I say.

My father nods and pours the water. "I'm sorry if it's not everything you hoped it would be."

"There's no problem," I say. "I'll be going back. Everything's fine."

"Does he treat you well?"

"Of course he does." I don't know why it would feel like a failure to have come back to say I was unhappy, or at least wasn't ecstatically happy.

Someone has been lying to me. I take a tiny sip of too-hot tea to give myself a moment. I've run through it over and over, and can only believe that my father would lie to save my feelings, familiarise me with my fate, if he couldn't alter it. He didn't snare the river man for me.

"You don't think he wouldn't treat me well, do you?" I ask, genuine and devious in equal measure. My father slips into the old storytelling posture, and I can see the time that has passed and the changes which have taken place since...since when? Since he started telling me those bedtime stories? He changed like the river, slow and constant and beside me. The distance now, between this posture and that, with the larger, fuller outline of him visible around his greying edges in my mind, is like the way the city changes, sudden and jarring.

"You don't want to hear those old stories," he says, "and you a grown woman."

"Why wouldn't I want to hear about the person my husband

was before we met?" I ask sweetly.

"You know him much better than me."

"What did he say when you offered him marriage to me?" I ask. My suspicions are piling like leaves.

It's his turn to drink his tea. By the way his eyes look over the rim, half-shadowed, he knows I suspect something.

"Was he pleased?" I ask. "Was he grateful? Has he ever thanked you?"

"Flower," says my father, "just tell me what's happened."

I am telling him; he just doesn't understand. "Did he ask for me?"

"Did he what?"

"Who made the offer?"

My father looks more comfortable at that, and the more at ease he seems, the more sure I am that he's hiding something. "He thought he did, all right," says my father. "That's the only way to handle someone like your husband. And not bad advice for marriage either, if I say so."

Perhaps not. And it's tempting even now to fall back into that narrative, when we were on the same winning side, where my clever father outwitted the river man to make a superb match for his beloved daughter.

"But did he ask for me?" I ask again.

"He didn't know about you to ask," says my father, an easy enough sidestep. "How could he have?"

"What did you do that he needed to feel he'd got the best of you?" I ask.

He laughs. "What did I *do*? He's a strange beast, is your husband. His rules aren't ours. You must know that."

Your kind can't be trusted. My species or my family?

"I see you've learned that lesson," he says.

His battle of wits was haggling a price.

"Have you offended him?" he asks.

"No." A pitiful lie.

"No shame in it," he says. "Like I said." He gives a sort of shrug which encompasses everything he means; the strangeness of my husband, our inability to see his lines before we cross them. Perhaps I'm just reading into the gesture things that make sense to me, adding a sentence or two to some other story I'm not even aware is being told. That's always been my father's way, to give you enough narrative control that whatever you fill those gaps with will seem utterly natural to you, common sense.

"He's good to me," I say. Is he?"I'm glad to hear it."

He will never tell me the truth. I know this. He'll change the subject, squirm out of my questions, simply lie. How do you make someone tell you the truth if they don't want to?

I don't stay in town long.

Relief again as I get back to the river, where it smells young and full, damp and green after all the smoky smells of the city. Relief tempered with a little disappointment, a little resignation, the same way my relief at being back in the city was mixed with unease. I might never be truly happy in one place again.

My husband's skin is scaled today, grey-green and black, and I find him spread on the rocks where the sun shines the strongest. Again I feel that urge to touch him though I know I shouldn't. Not just because he's a wild thing that doesn't belong to me, but because of everything else.

His scales shine dry and smooth in the sunshine. I've never seen him here before, or scaled this way. Usually his scales are sharp and thin, fish scales. As he matches his meals to all the shapes of his mouths, perhaps his shape brings out other things in him, undertones and highlights of his deep and constant mood.

Unsatisfied with my father's evasive answers in the city, I do the only thing it makes sense to do. I ask my husband.

"Do you remember my father?"

He looks at me with his snake eyes, slit-pupilled and shiny the way a stone can be shiny. "Yes," he says.

It's a bad habit, awful, really, how much of my perception of him is made up of expectations unmet, the things he doesn't do rather than those he does, the things I'd anticipate from anyone else but him. Anyone other than him, for instance, would have been sure to let me know that they valued the experience of meeting my father particularly, because I'm their wife.

"He didn't outwit you, did he?" I ask. "You punished him."

And I add, because I can't expect my inferences to be understood, "Why did you need me?"

"I didn't."

"Why did you accept me, then?" There's no point in being offended by the river.

"He broke my laws," says my husband. "Over a long period of time, until it was impossible to ignore."

I'm trying not to show how this unsettles me. "He told me he only met you once."

My husband nods his agreement slowly. "He only met me once."

He didn't realise that every time he saw the river he saw my husband. "What did he do?" I ask, dry-mouthed.

"That is between me and him." A predictable response.

"So I don't deserve to know what I'm atoning for?"

"There is no atonement. I didn't ask for him. I asked for you."

"I clearly have some purpose."

"Purpose, atonement, these are your words. I have none for them." Filmy eyelids slide over my husband's eyes. "He took more than he needed. He left only damage. I won't show you the scars. Don't ask to see them."

It comes as a surprise to think of there being parts of him I'm not meant to see. He walks naked. I thought that this aspect of him at least I knew. Even after the encounter with the wolves among the alders, when he showed me just how easy it is for him to send me where he wants me to go.

"That's a crime," I say quietly. "What he did."

"It's between us."

His actions have put me here, though, haven't they? I'm the end of a long sequence of other people's businesses. Duty settles on me, and dread. "What should I do?" I ask.

His mood shifts slowly beneath the surface like currents blowing sand at the bottom of the ocean. I can almost see them. "Nothing," he says, uncomprehending. As though it has never occurred to him even to expect help.

I open my eyes to nothing. There are no lights here to cheat the night. The air is full of the sound of running water downstairs; it takes me a moment to unravel it. Has the house moved while I was sleeping?

Regardless, I'm warm and dry. My bedroom door is closed. The water keeps running, and it doesn't take much to pull me along with it.

In the morning, I step down into a dark gleaming skin of water that covers the floor and laps halfway up the chair legs. There's no way but through it and my feet grow slow and stiff with cold after just a few steps. Some of the furniture is upended, as though the ocean tide came surging in and sucking out.

The water licks icily up my legs the faster I walk, reaching fingers up my calves and daring pinprick touches up my thighs. It feels like old fairytales and saints' bliss, the shock of it, the shivers.

When I open the front door the water all drains out in a rush, as though this ordinary house was perfectly watertight. My ankles are drying and my toes still numb as I watch the water seep away, running in narrow, determined streams that branch through the grass rather than sinking immediately into the soil. I follow it a few steps, still a little raw from sleep and all my higher judgements lying discarded on the floor of my bedroom with my clothes.

The streams begin to converge, and only then, knowing I'm close, do I begin to wonder whether this is a good idea. He was unsettled last night. Unquiet. I can't imagine him as a wave, roaring from wall to wall and tossing chairs on his foaming crests like boats. How quickly did he flee to leave so much of himself behind? There are so many tiny cracks he could have slipped out of had he wanted to. Then why stay? For me? Then why leave?

Drops of him trickle down my shins.

I follow the streams of water to the rocks and watch them run like glass ropes into the river. So this is how he feels today. I find a comfortable place to sit on the stones, close to the water, and lower my hand in. I'm imagining it because I'm only human, but I almost feel the current flinch at my touch. Sound travels well in water, I think. I hope he can hear me through my bones.

"I'm sorry for bringing up a painful memory yesterday," I say to the river. It feels good to say. Maybe because he isn't here looking at me, answering, interrupting. So I go on. "I didn't give my permission for any of this. I suppose no one does." I let my sleepy lack of boundaries carry me a little further. "You didn't either."

Part of me thinks this will do it, that I'll get to see him coalesce out of the water and take shape before my eyes. But at the same time it's not much of a surprise when the river just keeps on running past me.

"I want to be what you hoped I'd be," I say, but the moment's gone. If I didn't get him then I won't now. "I'll see you at dinner, I hope."

It is, as ever, unsettling to see him wear a woman's body, but I'm only relieved to see him at all tonight. He sits opposite me, shimmering in the warm evening light like gold on a streambed, and lifts his soup bowl to his lips.

He's larger than me in every way, built to a different scale, and strong. His arms are thick and his thighs muscled. But he's a swimmer, so the lines of his body are softened by the fat all water mammals need. It's hard not to be intimidated by how perfectly made he is, impossible not to compare myself to him. Perhaps the other animals and birds of his river feel the same, lusting after him or spurred to rage by instinctive rivalry.

"I hope I didn't disturb you this morning," I say.

"I was only waiting for you to get up."

"What for?"

"I wanted to see if you minded the mess I made."

If he was human I'd ask, coyly, why it mattered what I thought. "I was only sorry for upsetting you," I say instead.

"You did nothing."

"No," I say. "I did nothing. I did nothing when I should have done something."

All those years.

He doesn't understand, but that's fine. There are rules about being in relationships with other human beings, sensible ones, about boundaries and responsibility and taking care of yourself first. They don't apply here. His human shape is no disguise. He doesn't own this land, he is this land. He can't take care of himself, but he can take care of us, the warblers and otters and herons and me. And we can take care of him.

"Some things can't be fixed," he says.

"I don't believe that."

"And you're so small."

"That's no excuse."

His eyes focus on me. I wonder if this is the first time he has ever looked at me. I certainly feel like it is.

"You don't have to show me what he did," I say, "but if you don't, nothing will change." I know he doesn't like the thought of not changing, stagnant water and being stuck in one shape. Time is change and therefore time is life. Change is life. Life is change.

"And if I do?" he asks. His shape changes his voice a little. It's still him, but the throat from which it issues makes it higher, warmer.

"I can't promise," I say, "but I'll try. *Something* will change."

He can't go on living this way. Neither can I. His borders are already so tight against the encroachment of the city, slipping past the sprawl in optical illusions, his ways hidden behind tree branch angles. How much of him have we stolen already?

"It could change for the worse."

It could. I don't want to believe that it could. "Tell me what to do, then." There must be some ordeal, some ritual, some series of symbolic actions which will help.

"There are rules," he says. "I can't tell you what to do. I can't tell you how your actions will change things."

He is a river. His human voice is no disguise for that.

"I accept your terms," I say.

"There is nothing to accept," he replies, because he still doesn't understand how humans work.

He will open himself to me, every inch of his bank. I will be free to wander and see what is there, try to find what has been done to him.

I'll need all my cleverness, all my knowledge of my own father to try to root out the places he despoiled. I will do something, even if all I can think to do is pick up litter from his banks. Even if all I can do is respect a place I shouldn't go.

He chose me, and now I choose him.

My bedroom door stands open onto the landing, and with my head on the pillow I hear soft sounds of running water, and then quiet footsteps. My body rolls as the mattress sags beneath him, and I move aside to let him in.

Danielle Jorgenson-Murray is a Teesside-born video game translator based in Frankfurt. Her short fiction can be found in the *Cabinet of Heed*, *Dear Damsels*, *The Colored Lens*, *Ellipsis* and *The Future Fire*. She can be found tweeting at @ukenagashi and opining about books she's read at www.sparrowdove.com.

From the Embassy of Leaks to the Court of Cracks

Catherine Rockwood

We are sorry for the way this will arrive,
damp and damagesome. No doubt
the peculiar constitutions of our nations,
catastrophically susceptible to each other,
account for the long gap in correspondence
though here we find no record of any sort
to suggest a former, well-established channel.
That is, however, the way of our state;
we operate, as you can see, impromptu,
with agents very liable to defect.
Many have lived for a long time among you,
on a favorite shirt or as a way of thought
that landed on you suddenly and stayed.

Staying, as we hear, is something rare
within your fissured borders. Much tips out,
much topples. Much is built and clutches up
from treble-bound foundations, tenoned, splitting.
In your case, pride defers, takes second place
to the almighty fall. And how you love it!
The moment brickwork tears like rotten curtains;
the sound of earth exhaling after thunder
as brightness rushes back over downed walls.
For generations we've exploited this,
have learned both how to enter and to cling
to what you're always opening. We stuck
and slurred your symmetries. It was enough.

But recent changes, so oppressive for
both you and us, have forced this Embassy
to use newfangledness. To be overt.
We'll spell it in black mold, with feeling: PLEASE,

please tell us what would tempt you. Gasoline?
Redcurrant jam? A shattered whisky fifth,
muddled with builder's earth? Take them. Take these.
Make it official; all we have, we'll share.
Unerring knowledge of the passage *through*
is given us, which we will give to you
for love, and just one fractured future sight
of years to come. Friends, what we're saying is,
please tell us everything we shouldn't know.

Catherine Rockwood lives in MA. Poems in *Lady Churchill's Rosebud Wristlet*, *Liminality*, *Psaltery & Lyre*, and elsewhere. She reviews books for *Strange Horizons*, spends a lot of time chasing after three stubborn children and trying to get them to read fantasy literature, and depends heavily on coffee, gardening, and her poetry-writing group.

The House

You Cannot Return to the Burning Glade

Eileen Gunnell Lee

Trail Diary, Day 377

Birds: Barred owl, still and silent at the top of the old oak. Chickadee on her buckthorn branch at the edge of the clearing. Waiting for me and my pocket of seeds.

Animals: None to be seen in the trailcam frame, but hoof-prints in the mud by the creek. Deer. A big buck by the depth of the imprint.

Notes: I couldn't walk the trail today, not after the call from the hospital, and later with the funeral director. I stood at the door for a long time, breathing in what scents the wind sent me—sticky pine resin, leaf mould, and somewhere not far off, the black tar of roadwork. I couldn't move past the front porch. Couldn't bear even a quick jaunt, the trail so close to home. Feeling too much like I might miss an important phone call—might miss news of you. But those days are over. So I watched the trailcam, curled up with my laptop on your side of the bed. With my head on your pillow. It still smells like you.

Trail Diary, Day 379

Birds: A crow, worrying something on the chickadee's tree. Some small bit of a scavenged kill, lodged between branches. Kept the camera trained on it for a long time, remembering those videos we used to watch of crows using tools, how delighted we were by each quizzical cock of the avian head. Like they would figure out this whole messed up world given enough food pellets. Remember how we tried to lure them to the yard with peanuts, hoping they would leave something in return? Today the chickadee is nowhere to be seen.

Animals: A grey squirrel crossed the frame, but stayed on the far side of the creek. Skirting the bank as if avoiding something. Maybe a snake's hole. New deer tracks in the mud.

Notes: Still in bed. Still with the trailcam. I will make myself get up tomorrow. Eat something. Cross the front porch and stand in the sunshine, no matter how it burns. Remember when we would stay in bed all day? We'd lie so close, nearly every part of us touching—toes, knees, bellies, noses. We breathed each other like our lungs were connected. Ate only because we thought we had to. Because somewhere beneath feeling we knew that love could not sustain us forever. It was one of those times you looked me in the face—inches away, I could taste your breath. You said, "I'll come back for you, Dee. I'll give you a sign. Believe me." And I did. I do.

Trail Diary, Day 383

Birds: Chickadee was there on her branch, and came to my hand. The weight of her on my finger was almost too much. Her little claws too piercing. Feathers too delicate, brushing my open palm. Watched her eat seeds, tears streaming. Crow-calls a mile off.

Animals: None. No fresh prints on the bank. But there was a deer leg—lower-half, burnished fur to the ankle, gleaming bone and red muscle intact—wedged into the Y of the tree. Probably eagle-dropped. Should have included this in the bird list above.

Notes: My lungs burn with exertion, fresh air. Feels like it did during the fires last year, when we could barely breathe outside at all. Maybe it isn't the air now; maybe I will never be able to breathe again. Maybe this is how you felt?

Trail Diary, Day 385

Birds: The shadow of a host of sparrows crossed my bedroom window.

Animals: Trailcam is open on the desktop, sound on. Red squirrel scolding, marking some disturbance. I can't look.

Notes: In bed again. Since being out on the trail yesterday, every shift of light, every breath of pine or juniper carried on the wind, every sound seems to trigger some remembrance. Something I swore I'd forgotten comes to me through the chatter of a squirrel's teeth. The shape of the light through a clutch of maple keys. We tried to tap a few of those trees out past the glade in our second season, but in the drought the previous summer the trees drew the sap deep, keeping it for themselves. We didn't know the state of things. Thought we'd just done it wrong. We laughed about it in bed later. Laughed so hard we cried, a bit drunk on that sour elderberry wine the neighbour brought. And on possibility.

I kissed the tears from the corners of your eyes and I meant it.

But is this what you meant for me when you threw the rope up over the branch of the biggest maple? When you threw yourself back down to earth? Or did you intend, instead, a warning? Let not your step grace this patch of grass. Lest you remember.... But you didn't die, love. Not right away. Not for weeks.

Trail Diary, Day 386

Birds: Turkey vulture overhead the whole way from the house to the chickadee's glade. Not yet, not yet. No chickadee, but bluejays were screaming from the pine grove up the hill.

Animals: Three days ago I recorded that some bird had dropped a deer leg in the tree but now I'm second-guessing. It's a whole leg, nearly to the flank. How could I have missed that? A whole deer leg in a tree is not something easily missed. But I missed it. I must have. I must have missed it like I missed the ways the land was changing—the months of drought, insects I'd never seen before. I must have missed it like I missed the signs of your illness—your breakdown—because I didn't want to see? A deer leg needs a damned big eagle to carry it away. Or a cougar? I don't see mention of cougar prints or scat in the diary. I would remember that.

Notes: The diary reminds me it's almost time to do the backburn again. How I will do that without you, I don't know. That first year, when we didn't do it—we didn't know—how could we have known?—the fire came so close we had to turn the hose on the porch rails. Stay up all night to keep the wood wet. You fell asleep in your chair, hose running. Woke up screaming at me to get into the pond. To save myself. Wide awake but still dreaming, you couldn't fathom—couldn't see—that the pond was bone dry. Was that the first season I noticed a change in you? When we lived in the city it was easier to put these things aside. But when we found that doe caught in the fence, her head seared to the skull by some quick-burn wind, you weren't ever the same after that. After we walked the woods with your gun looking for all the half-burned souls. After that you mapped the fires. Tracked temperatures. Expanded your recording to the entire country. The continent. The world. The numbers were too much, too heavy. It was hard to breathe.

Trail Diary, Day 388

Birds: No chickadee on the trailcam today.

Animals: No.

Notes: Maybe it's the angle of the thing. Maybe I'm just going fucking crazy. But the deer leg's past flank now. Can I see shoulders? Black singe marks on the fur. It's moving. Back legs kicking. Trying to get free.

Trail Diary, Day 389

Birds: The chickadee is nearby. Calling and calling, but I haven't seen her.

Animals: Something is screaming in the forest. I can hear it with all the doors and windows closed. With our bedroom door closed.

Notes: I know what I'll see on the trail. I've seen it before. The tangle of stiff limbs. The singed fur. The skeletal mouth in a rictus of agony. The grid of teeth barring all mercy. Antlers like a lightning burn. Just like you said you would, you've come back to me, love. But you haven't left your pain behind. You've brought it back to life. You've given it new strength. And you leverage that strength between me and the world I live in now without you. The world I love. Even without you.

You cannot return to the burning glade. The burning world.

Tomorrow I'll walk the trail. Tomorrow I'll go out with your gun in my pocket. I'll bring extra bullets. But in the other pocket, I'll have the chickadee's seeds.

Eileen Gunnell Lee is a Canadian writer, educator, editor, and a PhD in English literature. She has stories published in or forthcoming from *Nightmare Magazine*, *Escape Pod*, *Selene Quarterly*, *Fusion Fragment*, and others. She is an Associate Editor at *Truancy Magazine*. As Selena Middleton, she publishes academic research on speculative fiction and ecocriticism and is Publisher and Editor-in-Chief at Stelliform Press, a new press for long-form climate fiction and non-fiction. Living halfway up the Niagara Escarpment in Hamilton, Ontario, she regularly meets deer, foxes, coyotes, cloaked riders on horseback, and mushrooms of ambiguous intent. She can be found on Twitter @eileenglee and on the web at specfic.vaults.ca. Stelliform Press is on Twitter, Instagram, and Facebook @StelliformPress and on the web at stelliform.press.

Facing Medusas

Liv Kane

One thousand apologies to my great-grandfather and the generations of fishermen I come from. I want to be an astronaut.

In the summer of 2019, a box jellyfish, known colloquially as the seawasp, stung the girl's left ankle. She had just resurfaced after a night dive and was stargazing, lying on her back and imagining the worlds miles above and below her. She'd turned the light attached to her gear off, remembering that all sorts of bioluminescent organisms fall for flashlights, when she heard another diver shout. She swam over, suddenly overcome by a weighty fear in the bottom of her abdomen. *Something's gonna eat me tonight.*

The largest of the cubozoans, the seawasp can grow up to two meters long, from the tip of its bell to the end of its longest tentacle. It possesses no brain, but rather a decentralized network of nerves, with a ring connecting its internal functions to the stimuli of the outside world.

In short, the deadliest animal in the ocean is a freeform bag of nematocysts and water. The Kraken and Moby Dick and Leviathan quiver next to this brain-less, poison-filled sack of jelly. Our minds, inclined to hyperbole and fable fabrication, could not make this thing up.

Most nights, when the rain is hot on my hands and I can feel a storm forming, I wish I could talk to Captain Zip. My great-grandfather passed a few weeks before I was born, after falling and hitting his head on the side of a cast-iron tub. The only person in my family who could tell better stories than me.

I want to ask him about the sharks he escaped and the seahorses he saved from his nets. About the billions of phytoplankton that danced beneath the *Miss Andrinna* and full moons. About how easy it is to lose yourself at sea.

I want to ask him why I wasn't born in the open ocean, scales and gills and tentacles more familiar to me than our neighbors and their mailboxes. My favorite songs are the gales made from hurricane wind and octopus breath. I know my amniotic fluid was all Gulf water.

I want Captain Zip to tell me about the barometric pressures and the sandbars and the schools of menhaden he loved, but most of all, I want him to tell me about the monsters.

It felt like kicking a bolt of lightning. One freestyle stroke and the girl had run into the deadliest creature in the ocean. Her leg seized up, and she shouted that she'd been stung. She was hauled onto the boat, her dive gear stripped, an entire bottle of vinegar poured on her leg. And then, her limbs began to seismically shimmy, the neurotoxins kicking in. The girl convulsed for six hours that night, falling in and out of a dream-state, imagining all the little harpoons digging through the skin in her leg and shooting up her bloodstream, into her heart.

She asked the woman she was with if she was going to die, without much animation. It felt like the proper, cinematic thing to do as they leafed through marine life guidebooks and tried to understand why her body was having such a bad reaction. Through the haze, it was determined that if she went into anaphylactic shock, she'd need to be airlifted. If she didn't, they'd let her body "ride out the poisons."

That night and into the morning, the girl wrote down all the people she loved in a bulleted list in her head. She imagined the different ways they might tell her story.

Unlike many of its cousins, *Alatina alata* has four eye-clusters with a total of twenty-four eyespots. Although scientists are unsure as to the connection between the nervous system and these eyes, they have concluded that the species reacts to dark shapes in its environment.

It's been documented that these sea wasps achieve up to four knots while stalking their prey, contradictory to the normal planktonic methods of most jellyfish. This is to say—the thing hunts. It is a predator. It belongs amongst our daydreams and our nightmares of the ocean.

This is to say—it was not a passive sting.

On those nights of cyclones, I think about how Captain Zip, shrimper and fisherman and father, turned down hundreds of mermaids for my great-grandmother. He believed in them the same way I believe in aliens.

If there are no mermaids, I wonder what pearly, iridescent eyes he actually saw beneath those waves. What monsters clung to the bottom of his boat, painful barnacles too calcified to scrape off. I wonder what spell he fell under. If it's hereditary.

He fled to the ocean again and again and again. He passed before he could recount his monsters to me, before he could paint pictures on the insides of my eyelids before I slept.

On those nights I can't fall asleep, I want him to tell me the genesis story of his fear.

If she could do it again, the girl would drape herself in pantyhose and stay far away from the flashlights. She would swim with her legs parallel to the surface instead of straight down. She would keep her mask glued to the water, not the stars.

But even now, she knows she would ignore the tiny voice in her gut, the one whispering of her trespass in a world she doesn't belong in. The one silently screaming danger.

Since humanity first began telling stories, we've been fascinated by the predators that remind us of our place. The mountain lions and tiger sharks and sea snakes and grizzly bears that have prowled the shadows of our cave drawings have also been the evils of our oral histories, and despite the growing separation between man and nature, we are still, today, fascinated by the creatures that could kill us.

These beings dictate a story we are not familiar with, one in which we are no longer the center of everything. With them, we are a cog, a part of a chain, reminded of the dirt within our blood. We revere their power and fear their potential. We give these creatures more legs and spikes and slime and poison until we have something that makes our hearts pound at the mention of its name. We mix their stories with our own.

They become the monsters of our God.

Most days, she thinks about Irukandji syndrome, the long-term effects of envenomation by box jellyfish. About cardiac arrest and hypertension and she convinces herself she has an enlarged heart for more than just emotional reasons. She thinks about her favorite Irukandji symptom, *a feeling of impending doom*. She wonders if that's truly just reserved for people on the verge of death, or whether we all feel those effects. Impending doom. Our fear of the end.

A brief glance at the final pages of the narrative.

Despite the seven-inch constellation on the back of my leg and the phantom shakes I get when my nerves set in, this girl returns to the ocean again and again and again. She stares for hours into the salt water and prays for the universe to open up to her, to let her explore the infinite blue-tinted spaces she needs to be a part of. She retells the fish fables that run through the estuaries of her family.

I must admit that my gulf swims are a little more hesitant now. I wade out into the water with my eyes on the surface, shuddering at the shreds of plastic bags and Sargassum seaweed that climb up my legs. I think about the slippery things that rule the waves, about how easily I could be taken under.

Once ashore, I grapple with my strange fondness of this unknown, my odd comfort in the places that speak of everything but safety. About my need to fill the empty, terrifying spaces with story.

Tonight, with my fingertips dipping into waves, I imagine what I'll tell my children when I get back from space.

The unbreathable air. The deep, unblinking abysses. The edges of matter that expand and contract like tides. Alien creatures that stalk our shadows, beings that look at us the way we look at them.

I decide that when typhoons touch the edges of our town and my children climb into bed with me, I will tell them that they have inherited the best parts of storytelling from Captain Zip. I will promise them that they will grow into their craving for danger, just like their mama.

With their warm fingers wrapped around mine, I'll tell them the story of a girl who almost died at sea, just looking for a place to be weightless.

Born and raised in San Antonio, TX, Liv Kane was first published by Young Pegasus Poetry and served as the inaugural Writer-in-Residence at the San Antonio Public Library. A current Kenyon Review Intern, Liv studies English, Film, and Environmental Studies at Kenyon College in the hopes of pursuing science writing post-grad. She received the New York Life Award for her poetry in 2019, and is the current Nonfiction Writer for Sunset Press. She is excited to share her new nonfiction collection, *Gulfwater* (Sunset Press, Spring 2021), with the world soon. In her free time, Liv draws deep sea creatures, photographs everything, and pretends she's near the ocean.

Ash and Scar

S. L. Harris

The last goodbye Simon had to say was to the tree. It had been a while, but he knew where to pull off the mountain road and knew where to walk sure as a dog going home. The old hills rolling without a spot flat enough to set a dinner plate, the twitching sounds of birds and squirrels, the sky the color of old jeans tossed over the June canopy: leaves of maple, basswood, and the ash. When you knew what to look for, the tree was hard to miss: white ash, split down the middle twenty-four years ago and bound back together. Simon set his hand against the scar. Smooth and pale and tall as a seven-year-old child. He felt, as he always did when he came here, a twinge in his legs. A memory not of pain but of absence. The question came to him again, as he traced his fingers up and down the scar, of whether a tree remembers, and what, and how.

Thinking of memory, he thought of Georgie, who had already soaked up half of his goodbyes, and would keep needing them, he was sure, long after Simon was gone. The tree, at least, would have nothing to ask.

His hand crept spiderlike away from the scar, to the rest of the trunk, the deep diamond grooves, and he was struck with the sense that these too were scars, that everything, after all, was a wound healed over.

Simon had said: "Now, Georgie, you take your medicines, you listen to your sister, you'll be OK. I've got your prescriptions at the CVS up in Buckhannon. And you have my number. She has it too. I can talk to the pharmacist if you need, you hear? Any time you're feeling poorly, you just give me a call."

And Georgie, filmy-yellow-eyed uncomprehending, Georgie who'd lost one too many and now simply refused another loss, answered, "But you'll be here, won't you, Simon?"

"No, Georgie. I told you. Healthways is closing. I'm moving. I'm going back to school."

"Good for you! What's your course of study?"

Simon sighed, and told him again. "Nursing."

Georgie told the same joke. "Ha! Ha! You gonna get one of those white dresses?"

Simon pretended to laugh, again.

As he left for the last time, Georgie said, "See ya next time." And Simon said nothing at all.

His hands continued to walk the trunk, slipped on something, paused. He bent his head closer. Little holes. Capital D's, like the multi-mouthed smileys that Jen, the secretary at HealthWays, would send in her text messages—*Got another laundry call for you :D D D D.*

Simon frowned walked around the trunk, looked up and down. They dotted the whole tree, except the smooth skin of the scar. D D D D. As he stared at one of the holes, something moved inside. Then a tiny green jewel emerged, iridescent. The insect slipped out of the little hole and unfolded itself into the world, emerging as Simon had himself emerged, all those years ago, from this very tree.

When he was seven, pins and needles in his legs had turned to weakness, then numbness, then nothing. The doctors in Charleston couldn't figure it. His dad, God bless him, had wanted to take him up to Cleveland and "get it all worked out," Medicaid reimbursements be damned. His father, born in the woods 'til he knew every tree, the fix-it man, the know-it-all. Yelling at the doctor, the nurses, the Medicaid office, because there was nothing broke that couldn't be figured and fixed if you just looked into it long enough. But his mother was of the opinion that there were things that just couldn't be understood or repaired, that the world happens and keeps happening, and you make the path you can. So it was she who made plans to change the house, to get the wheelchair, to call the used car lot every week. And it was these acts, much more than his father's assurances that they'd "get to the bottom of it," that made him feel that it would be alright.

But then Aunt Barbara, his mother's sister, had heard. Crazy Aunt Barbara, who exploded in tears and laughs at every visit and made every sentence a shout or a sermon, so that she would have crowded his early memories even if it hadn't been for the miracle.

Aunt Barbara said that when her husband—God rest his soul—was a boy he'd had the Polio and they'd done what the old-time people did and opened up an ash tree and passed him through it, and then they'd closed the ash tree up and he got better too. The old-time people knew what they were doing, she said, and she was no doctor, but she was just telling them, just saying to them. "There's always ways," she said.

His mother had shaken her head and said that they weren't going to toss Simon through a tree, and Barbara had asked how the hunt for a van was going, and Simon's mother had retreated to the kitchen.

That night they went out in the woods under the big moon and the haunted trees, looking for the young ash. His father at Barbara's direction took a sharp saw and carefully split the tree top to bottom. Then he pushed the split sides of the tree apart and pulled him through. Three times, they told him later, for three nights, but it all ran together in his memory: the young tree split and straining, the hands pulling him through, the night sounds, the stars.

When they were done, they tied up the tree with twine and mud plaster, according to Aunt Barbara's direction, and his father said, "What now?"

Aunt Barbara, serene, confident, answered, "We wait. The Lord provides."

So they waited. He noticed everyone's feelings in the house but his own. His father's anxious pacing. Aunt Barbara taking up residence in their house, like an unruffled cuckoo, and his mother, exhausted and annoyed, saying to him after hanging up on one of her calls with the school board about getting a ramp installed: "Sweetie, it's not you that needs fixed, it's the world."

Every night his father would go out to the ash tree, try to see it healing, try to see some sign. Sometimes he would take Simon on his back, the chair no good in the woods. No good in the mountains, really, Simon thought, even now: the steep-grade gravel driveways, the double-wides with four stairs up to the front door, the narrow doors, nothing built to fit.

Now he knelt by the ash tree that had given them the miracle his father had wanted, that had knitted itself back together, healed over the seasons until only the scar remained, while little by little feeling and then motion and then control returned to his legs. He saw that the bark had come away in patches, and beneath, on the flesh of the tree, there were traceries like flung spaghetti, the wrinkles of a brain.

And with the thought of a brain came Georgie again. One of his first patients for Healthways when he came back from college. College, where he'd shot himself like a rocket fueled by rage after hearing a teacher grumbling about wasting all this time on a ramp they didn't need anymore. And then, instead of nursing school, he came back here, that same rocket fuel burning itself out inside him. Simon drove people to appointments, did laundry, made meals, checked blood pressure, made sure they took their medicine. Georgie was a big guy, the kind of guy about whom everyone's first statement was, "he's a worker." His kidneys had gone bad when Simon first met him, and he hadn't been quite able to understand what it was to have a chronic condition. "How long 'til I'm back on my feet again?" he'd asked. And Simon, fresh on the job, trying to explain, feeling embarrassed because after all, he'd gotten away with something, thanks to tree magic or whatever it was. "It's about management," he said. "No cure. It's just not giving up."

And that, Georgie understood. Even as the Alzheimer's started and then became the very fact of his existence, he understood persistence, stubbornness, just getting along. That's the one thing people like Georgie had.

Then they pull the rug out from under you anyway.

He went back to the road where he'd left his car and paced a bit until he had some cell reception. He waited minutes for a couple ages to load, then placed a call.

"Hello," he said. "I'm calling about a tree."

"Yes?" said the woman at the tree management company. "How can I help you?"

"It's an ash tree. There's some kind of holes in it. Looks like the leaves are dying too."

"Oh, ash borer."

"What's that?"

"You said little holes in the trunk?"

"Yeah, that's right."

"So that'll be emerald ash borer. You want removal?"

"No, I was wanting to see if I could save it."

"Sometimes that's possible. How much of the leaf cover is gone?"

"He tried to remember. "There's still leaves."

"Is it a mature tree?"

"Um, I don't know. It's uh, at least 30 or so."

"OK. So that could be a candidate for injection treatment."

His hands made the motions of insulin jabs, allergy shots, Narcan. He'd tried to make sure his patients would be taken care of. Done his best. Done what he could. What was he supposed to do?

The voice on the other end of the line was asking: "Is it a high-value tree?"

"High-value?"

"We usually only recommend treatment for high-value trees. Where on your property is it?"

"Oh, it's not . . . it's not on my property."

There was a pause.

"If it's on a city street, you could call your city council. Where are you located?"

"No, it's not on a city street."

"OK. Are you worried about spread to your property? We could still talk about removal. Are there other infected trees in the area?"

Simon looked around. He hadn't really looked at trees since he'd walked in the woods with his dad. For his dad they'd been were companionship, compass, calendar. For Simon, mostly, they'd become background. But just then he felt like they were holding up the sky. The little blossoms on the basswood, the light coming through the maples.

The voice was saying, "What you're going to want to look for is those little holes, missing bark, leaves brown when they should be green."

He started walking as the cell service faded, and he saw what he hadn't noticed before. Exactly as the woman had said: trees stripped of bark in patches, dotted with holes like those on his. Like these woods had seen some battle that no one had noticed. He went back to the road, called back.

"Yeah, looks like a lot of infected trees."

"OK. So do I understand right that you have a healthy ash on your property you want protected?"

"What? No."

"Sir, what do you want the ash tree removed for, then?"

"I don't want it removed. I wanted to see if you can help me save it."

"It's on public property?"

"Yeah, I think so."

"So the usual treatment is an annual injection by own of our arborists, but I have to tell you it's not cheap, and you have to keep doing it indefinitely. If it's on public property I'd suggest you talk to your extension service or...."

Again, Simon's mind drifted to Georgie, to all his patients: the injections, the dialysis, the physical therapy, the stained clothes, the pills heaped in their boxes organized by day. Management, mitigation, indefinitely. There's no making things right. Some things you can't fix.

The woman was still talking, blinking in and out of the spotty reception, talking about money he didn't have. Simon hung up, got in the car, and began to drive, looking back once or twice through the pack of boxes and laundry, everything he owned in the back of the old Corolla. His foot got heavy on the gas, the mountain curves coming fast, and he felt pins and needles in his legs. He saw Georgie's number flash up on his phone for a minute before service went out.

He braked hard, turned around, and went back to his pull off. No service there now. He walked back to the ash tree. He felt the scar again, saw another of the borers climbing out of its hole. He pulled it off and crushed it between his fingers. There'd have to be someone to take care of it, but he didn't have a job anymore. The clinic was closed. He had a scholarship to nursing school. He was getting out.

His phone rang, and he saw, miraculously, two bars. He picked it up.

"Simon," said Georgie. "Where are you? There's someone calling me, saying I'm supposed to take my medicines, and I said, Simon gives them to me."

Simon started to say again that he was leaving, that Georgie's sister would get his medicines, that his neighbor would check in on him, that that was who was calling, that he and everyone were just going to have to figure it out by themselves, that he wished it were different, but it was what it was.

He plucked another borer off the tree, and said, "Alright, Georgie. Alright. I'll be there."

S. L. Harris is an archaeologist, teacher, and writer. Originally from West Virginia, he lives in Chicago with his wife, two children, and faithful hound. When not digging in libraries, gardens, or ancient houses, he enjoys making music, cooking, and running.

Gingko Biloba

Riley Tao

In ten thousand B.C.E., a family of three made shelter beneath my branches. My family watched through the wild winds as they shivered together against the winter fury. I waited for their cooling bodies to nourish my grasping roots.

But with a fallen branch and a magic spell, they brought a shard of summer into the heart of the frozen forest, and I began to wonder if they would survive.

On the first day, they picked the berries from the bushes beneath the snow. In the first week, a child dragged a struggling rabbit from its warren beneath the frost-hard earth. By the time the spring rains came and the ground sang green, the family was four, and there was always something good to eat in the hut around my trunk.

In six thousand B.C.E., a village of six hundred made shelter around my family. The breezes and the roots buzzed with our curiosity. My leaves would never stop prickling with the smoke of yams and deer and berries boiling down, and at the heart of every winter, a blazing campfire would blunt nature's chill fangs.

It warmed me to my core.

Over the years, my leaves grew rich and thick, and ten thousand lovers wrote their faces on my skin. The children explored every inch of me, scaling my trunk, plucking my fruits, lounging in my branches, finding parts of me I never knew I had.

Each spring, a girl would climb as high as she could through my verdant, red-gold canopy, and each spring, she would fail to reach my crown. Her son never made it, and neither did her nine grandchildren. But I remember when a little boy proudly placed his hand on my head, and the echoes of his great-grandmother ran through him.

In three thousand B.C.E., the sky spat death upon our home. A shooting star fell to the earth, its heat swallowing us whole. The birds screamed and cried as they fled, and my shadow writhed and scrambled to flee the inferno. The bones of the villagers cracked and melted away, and my brethren tilted drunkenly, celebrating one last party before their fall. The wishes of all the lovers on my skin were torn from my bark, and the fires hollowed me out, leaving me ashen, scarred, empty.

My leaves would never stop prickling with the flesh of the children who had slept in my arms and the smell of the trees I'd grown up with.

In one thousand B.C.E., the bees had made their home in my heart, and even the humans stayed away. The fires had split me open, and in the crevice where my flesh once was, a hive was born. New-green seedlings, unmarred by ash, tried to grow around me—but I blotted out the sun with my drooping, swaying leaves, smothering them with my shadow. I was taller than them all, stronger than them all, fortified with the ashes of those who came before.

The little ones were not. They had no right to live on the graves of my family.

A few times, a child—always a child—walked up to me, wide-eyed. They'd run their enraptured gaze along my scars, or gape at my limp, dull branches. But when they got close enough to touch, the furious swarm I'd taken in would awake, and they'd back away—for a thousand stings would kill as surely as a meteor strike.

But children grow, and some remember.

In one C.E., a woman brought her family into the shadow of my trunk, and from my fallen limbs she drew a fire to feed her parents and sister. With a spit of roasted venison in one hand and a green-wood torch in the other, she walked towards me. The buzzing, pulsing insects inside me awoke, and venom and pain belched forth from my heart.

But she held her gift of fire out, and the smoke of the same deer that had walked here for millennia danced around my trunk, filling my hollowed body. Gradually, cautiously, she drew closer to my gnarled core, soothing the bees with her smoke.

Shadows lashed at her as the fire flickered, and through the haze the swarm blindly struck, stinging her neck, her arms, her face.

I waited for her body to nourish my roots.

But though the stings assaulted her, she stood immutable, determined, still. Gently blowing the bees from her lips, she whispered, "I'm here. That's all."

The torch she bore blazed down to her very fingertips, the bees wobbling in the air, until the fervent, pent-up buzzing quieted to nothing.

She laid a hand on my trunk, and the echoes of her ancestors sang through her.

In one thousand C.E., the humans hewed a grand town from the earth. The bees inside me had long since faded, and stray cats slept in the space the fires had carved. Spring graced my leaves with dew, and every slight breeze would send sparkling droplets dancing across my park. Fresh, young trees had arisen alongside me—far away enough that they would grow in their own right, but close enough that the children could laugh and play among our boughs with ease.

I shared my fruits with all who came, and they spread the seeds across the world.

Over the years, brick by brick, plot by plot, the town grew. The buildings quenched the sun, leeching the life from my leaves. The streets ran brown with refuse and offal, and their toxins seeped into the earth. The grass and dirt was paved over and built upon, eroding the hill I stood upon to a dim shadow of what once had been.

But the children still came.

In two thousand C.E., the city canceled the night. Neverending light spilled from every window. Rivers of people flowed around me, cloaked in gasoline and steel. The streets hummed and buzzed like the bees that lived inside me so long ago.

I wondered whose smoke could calm them.

I could tell when they were going to swarm. Whether in tree-hearts or city-hearts, bees are the same. Something had enraged the grandest hive in history, and the stingers were about to come out.

And come out they did. Humanity delivered the judgement of the stars.

The blasts were fire and darkness. Windows shattered. Lights vanished. People crisped into ash and shadow.

The city fell silent.

It pared me to my core.

In six thousand C.E., the lands had healed. Only crumbling ruins indicated that there had ever been anything but timeless forest here. The same berry-bushes still hid beneath the snow. The same deer still rested at my base. Even the trees around me were indistinguishable from me, for all the more years I held over them.

For a century after the city disappeared, a mournful winter consumed the world, the likes of which I had never seen before, and never would again. It tempered me. I rebuilt, rooting myself into the earth so firmly that it would be easier to move the mountains themselves than uproot me.

I saw the humans, from time to time—what was left of them, that is. They marveled at the single tree on a hill, ancient beyond their measuring, some touched with reverence, others with joy. They would reach out to touch my trunk, or pick the leaves I shed.

But I kept my fruits in the highest branches, and my lower limbs had grown too brittle to support humanity. The birds and the sky were the only visitors to my verdant canopy.

I swallowed my scars, one by one, with a patience that would outlive eternity.

In ten thousand C.E., a family of four took shelter beneath my trunk.

The winter had been rough, but I had seen ones a thousand-fold worse. The weary family, nearly overwhelmed by nature's wrath, shuddered in the cold and wondered what they could possibly do to survive.

The mother's answer was the ancient city, and she left in hope of finding some intact cavern there. The father's answer was the sticks and branches, and he raced against the winter cold to create a fire. The childrens' answer was to rest and dream, for whatever time they had left.

Riley Tao (they/them) is a Californian twelfth grader who has been rejected by eighty-five literary agents while seeking representation for their YA fantasy novel, and turned to writing short stories after deciding that maybe they should walk before they run. They spent six months updating a creative writing blog with short stories on a weekly basis at rileyriles.wordpress.com before deciding to focus on a second novel. They also love computer science and mathematics, and in their free time they play homebrewed RPGs and hug their cat.

A Song Born

Remi Skytterstad

I.

What do the ravenous settlers know of faith? Praying on their knees under wooden roofs, without the wind on their cheeks and the sky over their heads, away from the roar of the rivers and the whispers of the leaves? How much is their faith worth when they persecute and murder for a metal cross, in the name of someone who never joins them in song nor dance?

No. Water is not to be walked on, just as mountains are not to be swum in.

April 1695
Finnmark, Norway
Despite his mother's orders, Kvive ran out onto the snow-covered lake. The warming weather of April had turned the snow on top of the ice to sludge, and the flat light from the overcast sky of clouds turned the world in front of him to a carpet of whitish-grey, where you couldn't tell where the lake ended, and the sky began.

Kvive had snowmelt to his shins as he ran, a spray of water in his wake.

"Eatni!" he yelled to his mother as he ran. "Look, it's safe! Imagine the time we can sa—" His words turned to a shriek as he fell into a frozen crevice on the lake. The flat light removed all shadows, so he didn't notice the drop before it was too late.

He landed on his stomach. Stretched out like a starfish he gasped for breath on the thin and dark sheet of ice, and the right side of his face pounded with pain. Lines like broken glass shot in every direction from his body and the ice groaned beneath his weight, like old limbs stretching.

Web-like circles ruptured in the ice under the weight of his hands and knees as he tried to raise himself up, and with a *crack* his arms breached through the ice into the freezing water.

"Oh, biru!" he said.

And with another and louder *crack*, the entire sheet of ice burst and Kvive fell into the dark water.

He gasped for air as the cold weighed down on his chest. Every breath was a fight and he trashed and flailed as he gulped water until his thick clothes of reindeer fur and skin pulled him under.

Through the ice above, he saw dark silhouettes move when people gathered around the crevice. Some—stripped of their clothes—jumped into the water, but he had sunk too deep for anyone to reach him.

His screams turned to fist-sized bubbles as the light of the crevice got smaller and smaller as he sank towards the bottom. Kvive held his breath, his lungs burning, even though he knew this was it. This was how he died. His body would never be recovered, and his mother would cry each year they moved their herd over the lake, and his body would still rest at the bottom, the flesh picked away from his bones by fish and other creatures.

He looked up towards the light one last time, before he prepared to take a deep breath, to let the lake fill him, and let the depths claim him.

Then he heard a whisper, and a hum vibrated from the bottom; the faint and intimate sound of someone speaking close to his ear, and tiny bubbles floated past Kvive towards the surface.

Free your soul, the voice said.

The whisper and hum clung to his body even closer than his wet clothes.

Kvive did as the voice said, at least his best attempt at it. He closed his eyes and let his limbs fall loose; his arms and legs trailed behind him as he gave himself to the lake.

Eventually the tiny bubbles from the bottom pushed him from the deep and up towards the light. But whether it was the light the priests would preach about, or the crevice in the ice, Kvive couldn't tell, and he didn't care. Both were better than the bottom of the lake.

Free your soul, the voice whispered again, *you're still too heavy.*

How? Kvive asked inside his mind.

Let go.

Kvive gave in to his instincts, and his lungs took the deep breath they had been craving. The dark and freezing lake filled his body, and his chest burned with pain as everything turned to black.

Kvive fell in and out of consciousness as his lungs emptied themselves of water. His chest burned, and he couldn't see a thing, but he felt the warm and familiar comfort of being swaddled in thick reindeer furs.

Everything, and everyone around him, were quiet, only the trees rustled as the wind moved through the pine forest.

Then he heard his mother, "Oh, my little—" But a man interrupted her.

"*Shh,* or you'll scare away the small sliver of life that remains in his body," the man whispered.

"Can I at least remove the blindfold?" she whispered back.

"No, his soul is still on a knife-edge between this world and the other. We must warm up his body before we remove it. Get a reindeer, make an incision behind its shoulder blade and let the blood pour into a waterskin. Quickly!"

Kvive had no sense of time as he fell in and out of consciousness, and without the ability to see, he wasn't sure where he was, or if he was dead or alive.

Eventually someone raised his head and pushed a waterskin against his lips, and a thick and warm liquid was poured into his mouth. Kvive choked on the blood, and the waterskin was taken away. This process happened several times until he must have emptied the waterskin.

Beside him his mother mumbled a prayer.

"Eatni," Kvive said weakly, "am I alive?"

"Yes, my dumb and reckless little boy," his mother answered. "He says you're going to live. Thank God for that."

"I . . . I just wanted to help . . . we'd save so much time crossing the lake." Kvive fell asleep, but his chest didn't burn, and he no longer felt cold.

The second thing a Sami learns was that the *siida*—a nomadic community of families—moves only as fast as its slowest member, and it is up to the stronger and healthier members to help the weaker ones keep up the pace. That said, it wasn't unusual that the elders that were too old and fragile to keep up with the *ráidu*—the line of people and gelded reindeers and wooden sleds—were left behind to die alone in the snow.

Because the first thing a Sami learns is that the reindeer herd always comes first—even though you almost drowned in a lake the day before.

Kvive had known thirteen of these migrations, six completely on foot and skis, and they didn't get any less backbreaking as he grew, nor did the blisters on his feet and hands—or the frostnip on his cheeks—stop emerging, even as his skin got thicker. He was always wet and cold and tired.

One day had passed since his miraculous swim back to the surface, and Kvive already drudged in the deep snow on his skis. Above him, greenfinches teased him from the sky as they flew and sang. He wished he were one of them; their migration seemed so easy.

The *siida* rushed towards the snow-free calving grounds for their reindeer herd near the coast; they had to be there before the middle of May before the reindeer cows started giving birth.

But at least he had Sara to share the long and tiring way with.

"Don't you sometimes wish you knew how to fly?" Kvive asked Sara.

She was a girl the same age as him, and they had lived together their entire lives.

"Fly?" Sara asked. "Where's the fun in that? How would our parents torture us then if we could just fly away? Besides, a dumb boy like yourself would probably get himself killed against the trunk of a tree if given wings."

"Now, hold on—" Kvive started.

"Running across a lake in the middle of April, without even a pole to test the ice with." She shook her head.

"I just wanted to help. I am a man now, and I should be with the other men and the herd. Instead, I'm stuck here with the moss-backs and you women and those damned sleds."

"What do you mean, *you women?*"

"Don't twist my words like you always do."

"I can tell you one thing," she said and poked Kvive with her wooden ski pole. "No woman would ever run out on the ice like a bull in heat and almost drown herself."

"Quit fooling around both of you," Sara's mother snapped, "go help your mother at the back. It's getting dark and we still have a way to go."

Due to Kvive's attempt at crossing the ice, the *siida* had wasted a day beside the lake. The April air was getting warmer, but a thick carpet of white still covered the ground, only punctured by tall pine trees stretching to the sky. They raced the weather, and they moved from sunrise to sunset trying to outrace spring.

The past years they would have crossed the lake, but in the past years they would have arrived at the lake much earlier. The *siida* moved slower because the church had arrested every Sami they suspected of blasphemy. Every *siida* had lost people, but probably none more than Kvive's. It didn't make any sense of course. What other religions were there? It seemed more like another attempt to punish the Sami, for being Sami.

"Eatni, can't I ride in the sled, just for a little while?" Kvive asked his mother after he had helped her get one of the sleds free from the deep snow. He had after all almost drowned the day before.

"And tire the animal that's pulling what we need to survive?" Around his mother's neck, tucked into the *gietkka*—a hollowed-out cradle of wood, lined with moss and pelts—his little brother cried. "Just be glad you're not behind with the herd, watching for wolves like your father." She rocked the *gietkka*. "Or lying in your own piss like your brother."

"I wish I was behind with the herd," Kvive said.

"Hah, you think you do. You should thank God me and your father have not been blessed with more children, or you'd be there, and your younger sibling would be helping me here. You think this is hard work? Hah!"

"But do we have to hurry so much, the weather is getting warmer anyways...."

His mother sighed. "What happens when the snow is warm, like it is now, and then the weather gets cold?"

"It gets hard."

"Exactly, it turns to cuoŋu. The kind of snow that will cut your hand if you fall, the kind of snow that will hinder the reindeer from reaching the lichen they eat, the kind of snow that makes it easier for wolves and wolverines to stalk our herd."

Kvive's mother looked up at the darkening sky. "Not to mention how dark the nights are. Your father and the other men are already struggling to keep the herd safe without being able to see their own feet in front of them."

Kvive didn't respond; he always knew when a conversation with his mother was over.

A man snickered from behind.

"What are you laughing—" Kvive started. It was the old man that had been travelling with their *siida*. He had been with them since they started moving the herd from the permanent winter pasture inland, but Kvive had never talked with him; especially not after he had learned he was the one who poured fresh reindeer blood in his mouth and tied a blindfold around his eyes.

He had a dark-tanned and coarse face, from half a life inside the smoky *lavvu*, and the other half outside in the sun and snow, with deep furrows whipped forth by wind and hail and piss-freezing cold. A reindeer trotted beside the old man. It didn't pull anything, and all it carried was an oval leather bag. It was the only animal he owned; an ungelded bull older than seven years, a *nammaláhppu*. His coat was white as snow, except for his brown beard and black hooves. They never used a *nammaláhppu* as a draft animal because they were impossible to tame, but the old man seemed to have complete control of the animal.

The old man laughed again.

"Lost your words, boy? It's your voice that loses a language first, but I hope you still have it in your mind," he said, tapping his temple.

Kvive ignored the old man and his reindeer, which seemed to be amused as well.

Three days later, the warning of Kvive's mother came true. Winter had its last freezing breath of life before giving in to spring, and the soft snow turned to *cuoŋu*—the kind that will cut you if you fall.

It forced the *siida* to quicken its pace even more, and they moved long after the sun had set. And worst of all, it hindered Kvive from seeing Sara. She thought of him as just a boy, and he wanted to prove to her that he was a man, but that's hard when you are stuck behind in the *ráidu*, taking care of your little brother and helping your mother.

Instead, walking behind Kvive was the old man, who must be dim-witted. Apart from his blindfold and blood nonsense, the old man had been whispering in his reindeer's ear and laughing, frowning, or nodding, as if it answered, the entire day.

"Why are you talking with it for?" Kvive finally asked, unable to ignore the old man any longer. "They are too stupid to understand human language, you know."

The old man smiled at Kvive, like he had been waiting for him to say something.

"First of all," he said, "he's not an 'it'. His name is Gappas." The reindeer nuzzled his hairy snout in the old man's neck at the sound of his name.

"That's forbidden, you know," Kvive said, "using Sami names. And an unoriginal one as well, naming it after the colour of its coat."

They were not allowed to take Sami names, not that there were any Sami names for humans.

"Oh," the old man laughed. "I didn't name him."

Before Kvive could respond, the old man spoke again. "Do you know how the first reindeer came to this earth, Guivi?" Again, he didn't wait for a response.

"Before Beaivi—the father of everything that lives and grows—shone on this earth, it was a world without light or living things. Just a barren rock enveloped in darkness, like a pebble inside your fist. And as he blessed us with his light, the lichen our herd are dependent on grew, the pine and birch trees that surround us reached for the skies, and the places we fish from filled up with water. But there was nothing there to graze on what he grew, nothing to take cover beneath the trees from the snow and rain, and nothing to drink from the waters and rivers. So, on his rays of sunshine, the first herd of reindeer migrated to this world."

"But as the herd grew, all the lichen disappeared, so he sent down other animals to keep the balance. Wolves, bears, eagles, and wolverines. And when the scales tipped to the other side again, he sent us, the Sami. To control and protect the herds and thus, restoring the balance."

If the old man wasn't dim-witted, he at least was a lunatic. Kvive knew his religion as well as any other boy his age, and it was God, the father of Jesus, who had made everything, and made man—even the Sami—after his own image. Despite no paintings of Jesus looking like any Sami he knew. In fact, there's no mention of any reindeer in the Bible to the best of his knowledge, but he knew all animals boarded Noah's ark.

"Okay . . . old man," Kvive said, "can you ask your sun-god to help us make the night less dark and the snow less cold?"

The old man looked at Kvive with pity.

"Don't be sad about the moonless nights, or the sharp snow, Guivi. They are all there to keep the balance. If you want to blame someone, blame the ravenous settlers. It is them who killed our gods by forcing us to forget, and it is them who forced a new god on us that doesn't know our land or our people. And it is them who have stolen our best pastures and taxed us to beggars. Again, the scales are unbalanced, and I'm afraid there is little Beaivi, or any of our other gods can do. No, in the end, this will be our fight."

Kvive couldn't challenge the old man's point about the settlers. Despite his young years, the frustration from his parents around the fire in the *lavvu* at night was unmistakable.

"Who are you?" Kvive asked. "Who are you really? They say you told everyone to shut up when I was unconscious, and then you talked about another world and poured blood in my mouth."

The old man's face fell.

"I have said too much. Run back to your mother now before she starts yelling at me as well," he said.

Kvive started humming the song he had heard under the ice, under his breath, so only the old man could hear him.

The old man grasped his shoulders. "Are you trying to get us killed?" When the old man spoke, there was a shift in his voice; it resonated around him, like an echo bouncing off surrounding hills.

The sudden shift in manner made Kvive scamper back on his skis.

"Never do that again!" the old man said.

"But—" Kvive started.

"Never!"

Later that night there was a swift change in the weather. A warm wind from the south caught up with the *siida*, and in a day or two spring would be on its way proper, and the hard snow gone with it.

But that's not what woke Kvive up. A green light seeped through the smoke-hole of the *lavvu*, permeating the entire tent with its shine. Apart from the fading embers of the fire, it was the only light in the *lavvu*.

Kvive's mother and little brother still slept, and his father would be sleeping with the herd and the other men. Kvive threw a couple of logs on the fire to keep it alive until the morning, then he cleaned the smoke of the *lavvu* from his eyes and sneaked outside.

The entire sky was awake. Large rivers of green and purple moved in the night sky like ribbons in the wind. You aren't supposed to stare at the aurora—that's how kids get lost—but Kvive couldn't take his eyes off the spectacle.

You could see as far as you could hear a dog bark. Every *lavvu*, even Sara's at the other end, in the *siida* was visible; silver trails of smoke escaped towards the sky from the cone-like shelters dug into the snow.

The men watching the herd would have an easy time looking for predators and making sure parts of the herd wouldn't get lost in the night.

Kvive had known the aurora for as long as he could remember, but never of this intensity in colour, extent in size, and animation in its movement.

Then he heard it. A rhythmic drumming, and the faint sound of a hum, like the one he heard under the ice. It came from the outskirts of the *siida*. From the old man's *lavvu*.

Kvive walked towards the sounds.

Outside the *lavvu*—untethered—Gappas watched the sky, his normally black eyes now a vivid green.

"Hello?" Kvive whispered, but no one answered.

Kvive had to find out what was going on. The whisper and the hum he heard underneath the ice had never left his mind, and even though he didn't remember how he got to the surface, the sounds he had heard felt as real to him as the ground beneath his feet.

He took a deep breath and pushed aside the flaps of canvas made from reindeer-skin and entered. On the inside it looked like any other *lavvu,* with its fire—now just embers—in the middle, with reindeer pelts circled around it.

The old man sat at the far end—where the father would sit if this were a family *lavvu*—cross-legged with a big and oval drum in his lap. The drum had red drawings of Samis fishing and hunting, reindeer grazing, and wolves, bears and wolverines. At the edges it had symbols depicting snow, rivers, mountains, and in the middle a big circle with rays around it, which had to be the sun.

The old man's eyes were rolled back in his skull, and he gnashed his teeth as he moved his jaw back and forth. He hit his drum with a t-formed reindeer antler, and there was clanking from inside the drum. It sounded like pieces of metal.

Kvive turned to leave, hoping the old man hadn't noticed him. This seemed like devilry, and a young and innocent soul like his was valuable to the devil.

"Stay," the old man commanded. He stopped gnashing his teeth and his eyes rolled back to their normal brown, but he kept on drumming.

Then his hum transformed into singing. But not like any singing Kvive had ever heard; wordless sounds reverberated from the tip of his tongue, to the back of his mouth, and down to his chest.

Children of Beaivi, the old man sang.

Kvive looked up, and instead of the ceiling, the wide night sky stretched itself in every direction towards the horizon.

In the sky the aurora fluttered and danced to the sound of the old man's voice and the beating of his drum. Kvive didn't understand the sounds, but they grew in his chest, they danced inside his head, left a taste in his mouth, and they spoke in his ears.

"*Come,*" a voice whispered. "*Dance with us.*" It wasn't the same voice he had heard underneath the ice, but it felt the same, as if it came from both outside and within him.

"How?" Kvive asked.

"*Free your soul.*"

Kvive took a deep breath and closed his eyes, but nothing happened.

How? Kvive asked the voice.

Let go.

He took another deep breath, but he didn't close his eyes this time. He arched backwards and his eyes rolled back like the old man's as he gave in to his mind; which craved to leave, and like jumping in a lake, he left his body in the *lavvu,* and entered the sky.

From the sky the entire *siida* was visible, and its surrounding rivers, lakes, and mountains.

The old man wasn't singing *about* the aurora—he sang the aurora itself. With his voice he made it dance and move, and he brought Kvive with him.

For the first time in weeks Kvive felt rested. He felt comfortable and safe, like sleeping in the *gietkka* tied to his mother's shoulders and waist.

The song grew in his chest, and it made him feel whole, like the song was a piece that had been missing; like filling your stomach when you are famished or drinking from a river when you are parched. Except, until now he had always had an aching hole in his chest, a drought in his throat, and a wanting in his soul.

Kvive's body in the *lavvu* shook, and tears poured down his cheeks.

The old man stopped his drumming, and his song faded out. And like resurfacing from the lake, he was back to shivering in his own body, despite the warmth of the *lavvu.*

"What was that?" Kvive wept, his tears trailing in light streaks down his smoke-stained face.

"That was the aurora," the old man answered. "They only show themselves in the night sky when the sun is strong. And today I asked Beaivi if he would be strong for your siida, and let his children dance for us. But I would have never imagined they'd let you dance with them . . . most peculiar."

"Also," the old man said and pointed a finger at Kvive, "you are incapable of doing what you're told, aren't you? But I suppose this was inevitable . . . ."

"What do you mean?" Kvive asked.

"You heard it once under the ice, and now your body and mind will never stop looking for it. That's what brought only you here tonight, and no one else. Since you are bent on killing us, I suppose I have no other choice than to teach you before you do something really stupid."

Kvive nodded and brushed away his tears.

"What you heard was a joik. No Sami is whole without the joik in their life, just as no Sami is whole without the wind on their face, or their herd in front of them."

"I want to learn," Kvive said, "and how to use the drum."

"The drum is a rune drum. But you are not ready to travel to the spirit world, nor talk with the gods. One does not call on the gods on a whim."

Kvive's face fell.

"But," the old man said, holding up a finger. "I can teach you how to joik."

Kvive nodded again, but his face wouldn't smile even though he wanted to.

"But you must remember, Guivi," the old man said, and his face darkened again, like it did the night before. "The joik is forbidden, and just being seen with a rune drum is punishable by death. Perhaps a few of the elders in your siida will have heard of the joik, but they will not speak of it. If the ravenous priests and settlers knew what happened here tonight, they'd burn the entire siida down, your parents and all."

"Why do you call me Guivi?" Kvive asked. The old man had used that name many times now, and it had been nagging at him.

"Because Kvive is the bastardized and norwegianized version of your true name. Our true names are stolen, forbidden, and soon forgotten. And if the day comes when you reclaim your heritage and Sami soul, you will never want to go by the name given to you by your suppressors."

"Are you sure you want this? Remember, not a word of this to anyone, about what we have talked about or what I have shown you. Not even to your mother or that girl you're always chasing," the old man said.

"Yes," Kvive answered, reaching out his hand. He could never go back to singing hymns under a wooden roof again.

"Then introductions are in order, Guivi," the old man said, taking Kvive's hand with both of his. "My name is Huika, and I'm the last noaidi. It is a pleasure to finally greet you, Guivi. I have seen how you act without thinking, I think we'll become great friends. My name is Huika and I'm the last noaidi."

II.

Before the ravenous settlers we had our paradise. A paradise we broke our backs for, blistered our hands for, tasted blood for.

It was the ravenous who invented sin in our life; in our *joik,* in our names, and now in our language. It was them who said paradise is preserved for the afterlife; an afterlife they would give us if we didn't fight against their theft of our lands, our religion, and our song-filled souls.

We knew what blood tasted like, but it is them who showed us it was an iron cross.

July 1695
Finnmark, Norway
The fickle weather of spring, with its bouts of rain, snow, and hail, had given way to summer, but life this far north was still rough, and getting caught in the harsh weather above the tree line could still mean your death. The days were never-ending, where the sun circled above your head, never setting. It was a trade the Sami did with the sun, because in the deep winter, the sun never rises for two moons.

The summer had been anything but prosperous for the herd. The weather had been unusually warm, and the insects thrived; they produced larvae in the reindeer's nostrils, ate the fat in their eyes so they went blind, or dug into their backs which would result in their death when autumn came.

With insects like black clouds above them, the herd had fled higher up in the mountains where it was colder and windier, but where there is neither grass nor lichen for them to graze on. The frustration in the *siida* hung in the air like the smell of rotten meat. The settlers didn't care how many animals they lost, they would demand the same amount of tax when winter came, nonetheless.

Kvive's father and the other men were away for days trying to regain control of the herd. The herd, his father had explained him, is not something you can keep safe like a precious stone held in your fist. Herding a big flock is more like having a piece of ice in your palm; only with an open hand can you delay it from melting and pouring out over the sides.

Huika had spent the summer near the coast showing Kvive how to do small rituals and sacrifices, and where to do them, and why you did them.

"See that?" Huika asked Kvive. They sat on a reindeer pelt laid on the ground, while Gappas grazed on the white lichen that surrounded them.

"Yes," Kvive said. He watched Sara feed and talk with the gelded reindeers.

Huika sighed. "No, not Sara. Do we have to do this every day?"

Kvive would rather be watching Sara than listen to whatever Huika wanted to talk about today, probably another lecture about the god who lived beneath the fire. Kvive and Sara were like family, but then again not by blood. It wasn't unusual that people in the same *siida* got together. That gave him hope.

"I'm talking about that!" Huika pointed to a couple of the elders in the *siida* who greeted the ground, as they exited the *lavvu* after waking up.

"Hello, mother ground and lands on which we live," they said, pouring out the rest of their blood gruel, which they drank to wake up in the mornings.

Kvive nodded. This wasn't new; it was something the elders did each year in the summer. Except they usually only did it at the beginning of summer, and not long into July. The herd was dependent on a successful summer, where the calves must eat and grow big enough in time for autumn.

"They have forgotten," Huika said, after another cup of gruel was poured to the ground. "It is the gods they are pouring their blood out for. They are asking them to take care of the herd, to help the calves grow."

"The gods? Like we've been doing?"

"Yes, but they don't know why. The knowledge of why they do it died generations ago. But this custom survived. Besides, blood gruel won't accomplish a task as big as helping an entire herd. That would require at least the sacrifice of a white calf at a sieidi."

Before Kvive could ask, Huika explained. "An altar for

offering. A place in nature that's so beautiful they must have been shaped by the gods themselves. It can be anything. A forest, a boulder, even an entire mountain."

Kvive knew about a place like that. He had taken Sara there a few times; a waterfall that always made a rainbow from its mist on sunny days.

"But we can help!" Kvive said. Even though they had arrived at summer pasture in time for the calves, he still felt bad for the incident at the lake. Besides, what was the point in learning these things if he couldn't use it to help those he cared for?

"If only," Huika answered, smiling sympathetically. "The things I have shown you are as far as I dare take it. Just the joik that we're practicing is putting all our lives at risk. If the ravenous found out that this siida made an offer of anything, they'd be after our heads for paganism and blasphemy, and they wouldn't stop chasing us until they executed the one responsible. You must know, Guivi. Me and you are to the best of my knowledge, the last who remember. And if we want to keep on remembering, we must be smart and stay alive, so that we can give away our knowledge, when the time is right."

Kvive didn't respond. All he wanted was to help his family and the *siida*. Autumn would be here soon, and then, the dark and deep winter.

Two days later, shouting in Norwegian roused the *siida*.

"Out from your tents!" a voice shouted. "Out, now!"

Kvive stirred on his reindeer pelt from the noise.

"Kvive!" His mother threw a lump of reindeer cheese at his head. "Kvive!"

"What—what is it?"

"Wash your eyes. I think a priest is here." She threw a skin of water at him.

Kvive left the dark *lavvu* still rubbing smoke from his face.

The priest was the tallest man Kvive had ever seen. He wore a black cassock caked with mud, and a white collar. Dark and wavy hair reached him to the shoulders, and around his neck hung a silver cross. It wasn't unusual that priests visited the *siida*'s—it was how the church kept the faith with the Sami as they moved their herds.

What was unusual was the armed soldiers behind him.

There were at least 20 of them, tall and pale men wearing black uniforms with silver buttons, with swords fastened to black leather belts. Except for one, who held an axe over his shoulder.

The priest spread his arms, the sleeves hanging like black wings, and he said, "I wish I were visiting you under better circumstances, my children. My name is Bishop Niels, but you might know me as Niels the Righteous." He had a soft voice, and his words left his mouth with the monotony of a stream.

Everyone knew about Bishop Niels, and he was anything but righteous.

"We are here on an assignment for the church and our king. We are looking for a man, and we hope you will be able to assist us."

Kvive's mother spoke, "The men are away trying to gather the herd, higher up."

"Ah, but the man we are looking for won't be running after any herd." The priest examined the crowd. "We are looking for a witch. A pagan. Someone who serves false gods."

Kvive's eyes widened, and he barely suppressed a gasp. But no one shouted or pointed fingers at Huika's *lavvu*.

Kvive's mother spoke again, "There are no men here left for you to arrest. That sounds like blasphemy, and we know the laws. Everyone in this *siida* are devout Christians and loyal subjects of the king. I promise you that."

The priest smiled at her, his face looked like the grimace a child makes the first time it tastes reindeer marrow sucked from the bone.

Then he nodded at the soldiers. "Look for him and look for anything . . . blasphemous."

Some of the soldiers worked their way through the *siida*, questioning the old men and turned every *lavvu* upside down. The rest inspected the surrounding area.

A scream from outside the *siida* stopped the search.

Shortly after the soldiers came back with a girl dragged behind them.

It was Sara, and she had blood all over her hands. "I'm sorry! I just checked if it was still alive! I just wanted to watch the rainbow, please!" She wailed and wept in the strong arms of the soldier.

Kvive looked down at his own shaking hands, they were still red from the night before. He had tried washing the blood off in the stream, but blood doesn't remove easily; and there was blood on the cuffs of his shirt. He hid his hands inside his sleeves away from the scrutinizing eyes of the priest. Sara must have gone to the *sieidi* alone. Kvive's mind was blank, and he had no idea what to do. What could he do?

"Sara!" Her mother ran towards the soldier dragging her daughter.

The priest ordered, "Bring the girl to me. And control that woman!"

A different soldier grabbed Sara's mother. He clamped his arm in front of her face, muting her protests and wails.

The soldier threw Sara to the ground before the priest. The priest put his arm around her shoulder and whispered in her ear. Sara shook her head and nodded at his words, before she pointed to the place she was dragged from.

The priest said to two of his men, "That way, find a white calf with its throat slit near a waterfall. Bring it to me."

A while later the soldiers came back with the dead calf in their hands. They laid it down before the priest.

The priest whispered one more question in Sara's ear. She shook her head. Then he nodded at the soldier with the axe. Sara got picked up from the ground like she was a stick doll and forced down on a tree stub used for chopping wood by her neck.

Kvive had to do something. Anything. "Wait!" Kvive screamed. "It wasn't her, she only checked if it was still alive. It was me!"

At the same time Sara's mother broke free from the soldier holding her and ran towards her daughter, screaming, "Sara! *Sara!*"

The priest looked at Kvive with lazy eyes and nodded at the soldier with the axe again. The axe fell and cut Sara's head off in one sweep.

Bewildered, and not knowing what to do, Sara's mother kneeled in the blood of her daughter that pooled a dark red on the ground. She grabbed Sara's shoulders and lined her body up with her severed head; she stroked her daughters back and heaved voiceless cries.

Some of the mothers started screaming and shouting, others picked up their babies from the ground or grasped the shoulders of their elder kids to turn them around. A few of the mothers and older men ran at Sara's killer with their fists raised, but with little effort from the soldiers, the men and women were thrown, beaten, or kicked to the ground.

Kvive fell to his knees and hands. He tried to force out a *why,* but his voice failed him. His vision swam, and his body swayed, bile surged up in his throat and he felt like throwing up.

"Order!" the priest said. "There will be order!" Apart from the babies crying, the sobbing of the elder kids, and the people on the ground moaning in pain, it became quiet.

"You," the priest said, pointing at Kvive who still shook on the ground on his hands and knees. "You said it wasn't her."

Kvive looked over at his mother. Around her neck his brother cried in the *gietkka.* Tears welled up in her eyes, and she shook her head. Kvive didn't answer the priest.

"He wanted to save her!" his mother pleaded.

"We will continue taking lives," the priest said, "until someone points us in the direction of the witch. The last *siida* we visited saw three of their own die. Please, be smarter than them. That white calf is all the proof I need to execute everyone here, with the support of the church and our king."

"He doesn't know anything, please, he's just a boy!" Kvive's mother said.

"Bring him to me," the priest said.

Kvive's mother—with his little brother still in the *gietkka*—moved in front of Kvive to shield him, but with the hilt of a sword she got knocked to the ground.

"Eatni!" Kvive said as his mother fell to the ground unconscious, and his little brother cried, still tied across her chest.

A soldier grabbed and dragged Kvive along the ground, just like they had done with Sara, only minutes ago.

The priest laid both of his hands on Kvive's shoulders and stared into his eyes, as if looking for something in Kvive's brown eyes with his unnatural bright blue ones.

Kvive's bottom lip quivered, and tears streamed down his face. What had he done? Sara was dead because of him. And now he either gave up Huika, or he would die as well. Maybe the entire *siida* would be burned down, like Huika had warned.

"Have you seen that poor calf before?" The priest nodded towards the dead animal.

Kvive didn't answer.

The priest made a show of looking at Kvive's hands and shirt, and his eyes narrowed. "Do you know the punishment for paganism?"

"Death," Kvive said, swallowing a cry.

"And what about the witch, do you know him?"

Kvive shook his head, fearing his words would fail him.

Again, the priest nodded at the soldier with the axe.

Kvive kicked and punched around himself in a frenzy when the soldier grabbed him and carried him to the tree stub. "I hope you burn in hell, you bastards! In hell! Eatni! Áhčči!" he yelled at the soldier, and after his parents.

An elbow to his face silenced him; Kvive gasped for breath as blood filled his mouth. The soldier tore off his shirt, exposing his neck. Then he forced Kvive down on the tree stub. Sara's blood was warm and sticky against his throat, and the pungent smell of iron invaded his nose.

Why was no one running to his rescue? His mother was still on the ground unconscious, but everyone else just stood there, paralyzed. Some cried, others had their face turned away, and some watched with dead eyes; people Kvive had known his entire life.

"I'll give you this last chance, boy, that's more than I gave the girl," the priest said. "What do you know about the—"

A lightning strike in the distance interrupted the priest, and the westward wind that had been blowing all day stopped. And for a few seconds, everyone, including the weather, got quiet.

As abruptly as it had stopped, a wind blew in from the east; it grew fast in strength, taking every pelt laid outside, and clothes that were hung to dry, with it. Following the wind, black clouds roiled in over the mountains against the *siida*, like smoke from a fire that has been extinguished with water. The sound from the thunder and the flashes from lightning caught up with each other fast as the storm charged at them.

The priest raised his hand at the executioner. He lowered his axe to the ground but kept his foot on Kvive's back.

"Finally," the priest said, "we found him."

The wind roared in Kvive's skull and the rain whipped his face. Echoing around him he heard a drum and the clanking of metal.

Riding with the storm Huika and Gappas descended the sloped mountainside that overlooked the *siida*. With wide sweeps of his arm Huika beat at his drum with his t-formed antler. Like a cacophony of different songs, there were several *joiks* in different tones at the same time from the sky.

Children of Ipmil and Beaivi, the voice in the storm roared.

The song clung to Kvive's body with the wind and it roared in his head.

Unleash like a spring river, the voice continued in the sky.

The priest clutched his silver cross with both hands and said, "God will punish you!" He bent his head and mumbled a prayer, while making the cross on his chest. Raising his head again, he ordered the soldiers, "Seize him you cowards! Seize him!"

The soldiers exchanged looks, fear painted on their faces.

"Kill him! Kill the witch!" the priest ordered. "For your king and God!"

At that, every soldier ran towards Huika and Gappas, with their weapons raised, screaming like they were possessed.

Huika raised his arm and struck his drum with his antler.

Biegga! The sky roared. Gusts of wind slammed the soldiers to the ground.

Huika struck again.

Arvi! And the rain turned to fist-sized hail clobbering the soldiers huddling on the ground.

And again.

Álddagas! And a single bolt of lightning struck the executioner in the head. His head blazed like a fire, and fiery lines split in his face like cracked ice before he fell.

Gappas trotted towards the priest, not acknowledging the soldiers scattered before him and Huika.

A couple of meters away from the priest who still clutched his cross, Huika's eyes rolled back and regained their colour, and the storm and the wind died down.

"Leave," Huika said in Norwegian. "Leave now, and I will spare you the humiliation of reaching your afterlife because of what you call false gods. Leave now, and I will let your men live."

That was a fake threat. Huika had talked with Kvive about balance. The gods would only help take a life responsible for the theft of another.

The priest didn't respond. He turned on his heel and ran in the same direction they came from, his wavy hair and black clothes flailing in the remnants of the dying storm.

"I'm sorry," Kvive sobbed. He ran to his mother and little brother and buried his face in her arms.

"I didn't…I didn't know, what…oh, Sara. It's all my fault," Kvive cried to Huika.

Huika didn't respond, he just walked over to Kvive and stroked his back as he cried.

III.

The ravenous built prisons on our lands and called them churches. They filled them with our voiceless faces stripped of all colours of home and squelched the song in our souls. There, the rattan cane clapped over coarse hands, for not speaking their language.

We knew what it was like to hurt, but not the word for help.

September 1695
Finnmark, Norway
Cloudberries had coloured the ground orange, and the warm winds of summer had given way to the freezing wind of autumn. The gelded reindeers pulled the sleds on the bare ground over rocks and pouring rivers, as the *siida* moved inland towards the permanent winter pastures again.

Kvive had let the *ráidu* move ahead in advance. He sat on a boulder overlooking a river trying to *joik* Sara, as birds flew from tree to tree around him, and he drummed his fingers against his lap pretending it was a rune drum. Huika said that the best way to remember someone was through *joik*.

He waited for Huika to catch up with him. After the priest and the soldiers had run back to town, Huika had left the *siida* before he was chased away, but he still followed, knowing it was only a matter of time before the settlers came back for him. And the first place they would look was Kvive's *siida.*

"You're getting better, Guivi," Huika said as he and Gappas approached Kvive. "But you are still *joiking* about Sara. Tell me about her, how does she talk?"

Kvive thought for a few seconds before answering. "She talked fast, as if her mind outran her mouth. She would end a sentence before it was over, just to start a new one, and she'd answer her own questions as if she found the answer as she asked them."

"And how does she sound?" Huika asked.

"Beautiful. Carefree like the song of a bird."

"And what does she want?"

"What, how should I—"

"Just answer, don't think about it."

"She always tries to help those she cares for, even if—"

"Great," Huika interrupted. "Now, joik her."

Kvive cleared his throat.

At first his voice was barely audible, like the pitter-patter of a bird on a branch. Then it grew; the sound of his voice leaped, it went high and low and back and forth like a bird in flight. The *joik* was fast, and just when you thought you could follow it, or thought you knew where it was going, it started in a new direction, with new sounds.

Huika joined Kvive with his drum.

Kvive grinned as he *joiked* Sara even louder in time with Huika's drum, and in that moment, he was grateful for knowing her.

Above, birds joined them, both in song and in flight. They flew like they were one being, in a cloud-like pattern, to the tune and in time with Kvive's *joik.*

Kvive stopped when tears trailed down his cheeks. "Why are you teaching me this?" he asked. It was like a gift he had done nothing to deserve.

"Did you see her?"

"Yes."

"Exactly, I did as well. We remembered her. Not only her face, or her ambitions, but her very soul."

Kvive smiled at that and wiped his tears away.

"You see, Guivi, there was a time when the Sami were free as the birds above us, chasing the best pastures with our herds.

Now we step with care on our own lands, like beggars trying to cross a river without getting wet for a piece of stale bread on the other side. I had given up my calling as a noaidi before you forced me to remember again, by trying to kill yourself under that ice. And then, that night under the aurora, you heard our song, and you joined me in the night sky. You have given me hope again, and I am teaching you so that someone will remember when I am gone."

"You're not that old," Kvive said.

Huika smiled at that, the deep furrows of his face wrinkling around his eyes and mouth.

"I have seen the future," Huika said after a long silence. "It will become much worse before it gets better. But it will get better. You, and those you help remember will start it. We have already lost our lands, our names, and our gods. All we have left is our language, and that we must fight to keep to the very end. What do you think the ravenous call the snow when it melts and then freezes? We call it cuoŋu, and they call it snow. Or snow that has turned to coarse pebbles? We call it seaŋáš, and they call it snow. They have never led a life where the difference might mean the loss of a livelihood. And if we lose our language, we will lose our understanding of the world that makes us Sami."

Huika fell silent with a pained expression on his face, as if he weren't sure if it was smart to tell Kvive what he told him next.

"I saw the future in you, Guivi, that night under the aurora. And when the time comes, you won't be ready, but you will put your nose to the wind and do your best. And in the wake of your life, a new future for the Sami will start."

There was another long silence, before Kvive said, "I have to leave. Mother has been watching me like a hawk since we lost Sara."

"Just promise me you will remember what we talked about," Huika said solemnly.

"I will."

Kvive jumped from the boulder and ran after the tracks of the *ráidu.*

Kvive caught up with the *ráidu* faster than he had thought. Even though the ground was bare, this area was flat, and the sleds should have been moving faster.

In the distance there was shouting and movement.

The cause of the commotion were soldiers between the people in the *siida*. The same kind of soldiers that had visited them that summer, wearing black uniforms with silver buttons.

Nearly every man and woman in the *siida* had a blade to their throat. At the helm of the cluster, was the same priest from summer. Still as tall, and still as pale, clutching his silver cross as he talked with his soft voice. "Summon the witch, or we will cut every throat here and claim your herd as property of the church!"

The pleas of mercy, and the explanations that Huika had left them, were ignored.

"Summon the witch, or we will cut every throat here and claim your herd as property of the church!" he said like a chant, over and over again.

"Stop!" Kvive ran straight up to the priest, avoiding the hands of soldiers that grabbed at him. "The old man is gone. We haven't seen him since summer. Leave us alone!"

"No!" Kvive's parents protested, but with a fist to their stomach the soldiers silenced them. On the ground, in the *gietkka*, his little brother slept, oblivious to what was happening.

The priest smiled at Kvive, recognizing him. "Ah, but we got you. I think you will be of immense help." The priest nodded at one of the soldiers.

A soldier put a blade against Kvive's throat. The cold steel sent shivers down his back, but this time he didn't cry.

"You will tell us where the witch is, or we will hurt you in ways you thought unimaginable," the priest said.

"I don't know, and that's the truth. I swear it on the cross around your neck!"

"Your promises mean nothing to me, boy." The priest pulled out a knife from his wide sleeve. "I think we will start with your fingers. One more chance boy, before you lose a thumb. Where is the witch?"

"There," Kvive said, as surprised as the priest.

Moving at a slow trot, Huika rode Gappas through the mass of people towards the priest. He held out his arms wide while humming a song. None of the soldiers dared approach him.

"Careful, witch," the priest said, "one wrong move and my men will start cutting throats."

"I'm not here to fight," Huika answered. "I'm here to let it end."

"Oh, we can end it for you."

"It's only me you want. Release these people and I'll be your prisoner. You don't want to kill an entire *siida*. You might consider the Sami as beaten dogs, but hit hard enough, and often enough, and even a beaten dog might bite back. Or do you want repeats of the riots this land is bloodied with?"

Now the earlier conversation made sense. Huika knew this was the only way for this to end, and that was by turning himself in. But how could he do that? Kvive wasn't ready, what about all he hadn't learned yet? But knowing Huika, he probably had a plan.

Huika gave the priest a wide smile.

"Besides, I have the ears of many powerful beings, and if you break this agreement, you will know their wrath."

The priests face twitched. "Fine," he said. "Hand over your drum and we'll take you with us."

Huika dismounted Gappas and unclasped his leather bag. He handed it to the priest and turned his back to him, so they could bind his hands.

The priest whispered in Huika's ear, "Do you repent your sins, with all of your heart and body?"

"No," Huika said.

"Will you ask of me, on behalf of God, to forgive your sins?"

"That won't be necessary."

"Then you leave me with no choice."

With his knife still in his hand, the priest reached around Huika's neck and slit it. Huika fell to his knees, blood spilling from his throat, before falling face first into the dirt. Seconds later, Gappas stopped breathing, and fell beside Huika.

"No!" Kvive screamed in Sami. "Someone, please help him!"

But none ran to Huika's rescue, as if no one understood him.

Desperate to save Huika he roared, "Beaivi and Ipmil, take my sacrifice!"

Then he pushed his throat against the sharp blade and threw his neck along the edge of the sword.

Horrified, the soldier pulled away his sword from Kvive's throat.

Kvive fell to his knees, with blood streaming down his chest.

Guivi sat on a reindeer pelt atop a boulder, overlooking the *siida*. The first snow of winter fell around him like the tiny white feathers of a grouse's winter coat. He had regained most of his voice, and the wound across his throat had healed, even though it had been only a few days since he had tried to sacrifice himself for Huika.

The elders now called him *imašgánda*—miracle boy. First because of his miraculous survival in the lake, then his wound across his throat—a certain death—that had healed in a matter of hours. His sacrifice had done nothing, except scare away the priest and the soldiers, and hopefully they thought he was dead and wouldn't return for him. But his sacrifice must have been refused by the gods, so they gave him his life back.

Guivi started humming, and he drummed on the rune drum the priest had left behind as he fled the *siida*.

The sound of his voice resonated around him, like an echo bouncing off surrounding hills. It permeated the entire *siida*, and soon everyone, including his mother, father, and little brother, listened to him.

Then he *joiked* Huika.

It didn't have many words, but it filled the soul of everyone there, like a piece that had been missing; it felt like filling your stomach when you are famished or drinking from a river when you are parched. Except, until now they had always had an aching hole in their chests, a drought in their throats, and a wanting in their souls.

And for the first time in centuries, his people felt whole.

Remi Skytterstad is from Norway where he studies educational science. He lives with his daughter who attends kindergarten. He has poetry and fiction published in both Norwegian and English. His story 'A Song Born' is based on the real struggles of the Sami population in Norway. Find him on twitter @Skytterstad.

The Birds

when the coral copies our fashion advice

Ashley Bao

bleach blonde was the look of the summer:
colorless skeleton of polyps and aging fish spines.
rocks smoothly slate gray as salt water
grinds it down; it had no algal coat to protect and
nourish, no obsidian shelled mussels hanging off
the edges, beating themselves to the rhythm of the tide.

the moon rises and so the tide flows, warming waves
crashed, blue hypoxic seafoam gurgled a last
lament. when the seagull cried out for the last time,
it took the flock with it. once upon a time,
if you cupped blue with spread out fingers, either sky
or sea, you could observe life teeming in between your knuckles.

you can't help but paint old histories in pink watercolors:
take the brush, cover the blemishes, brighten the hues,
you don't know what parts are real and which parts you wish were.

a truth: bleach blonde did not stay after summer. girls found their
    hair
was too crackly, brittle from constant treatment. we started
thinking maroon silk was better than sulphureous wires stuck
to scalps with elmer's glue. life breeds life, their hair was already
    dead
but the reef still clung like a damsel in distress. if it was rapunzel,
it would've let down its hair for anyone, if only they'd climb the
    tower.

you replant a polyp, a seedling you nurtured to life, it is its
time to fledge. you lace your fingers together and
cautiously peer into the snowglobe you have shaken back to life:

tangs so bright they turn chartreuse
at noon, cinnabar anemones with squirming tentacles,
emerald seagrass plush to the touch. tilt your head,
and see the terns circling, wide white wings casting shade
as a warning. they are the most polite predators

you think you have ever seen; when smog clogged
city streets and winter air turned tepid, we sent
no heads-up: *perhaps this might be your last century;*
best prepare your trembling lungs, your hummingbird hearts, bleached
platinum is our new gold. painting the color back into
coral's white skeleton is our apology. we try so the message we
never sent will not come
true.

Ashley Bao is a Chinese-Canadian-American high school junior. She spends her time writing and dreaming, mostly about cats. Her poetry and short fiction have appeared in *Liminality*, *Strange Horizons*, *Cast of Wonders*, and elsewhere.

The Forest

Wash'ashore Plastics
Museum

Corey Farrenkopf

From the dock, the sandbar across the bay looked awash with shipwreck survivors dragging themselves from the surf. It was low tide. The bay was a mirror of sky reflecting off the green Atlantic. Corin guided his Boston Whaler through the shallows, hoping to ferry the stranded back to shore. He already called 911 and the Coast Guard. Their nearest boat was an hour out.

It was mid-May. Salt spray kicked up from the boat's prow. As Corin approached, he noticed the bleached white bodies were fixed in odd poses, hands on hips, rigid, fingers extended towards the sky. Some were inhumanly thin. Others were muscled like bodybuilders. Corin throttled down with the realization. They were mannequins, the same as any other debris ferried down the coast on the Gulf Stream.

Cutting the engine, he nosed into shore.

Corin gathered the mannequins like kindling, stacking each in the boat's bow. He returned for five trips. It was impossible to fit them all in one go. He couldn't leave any behind for someone else to mistake for disaster.

"What will you do with them?" the EMT asked, his ambulance parked on the overgrown lawn in front of the museum. The man had already radioed in to cancel the approaching rescue boats.

"Add them to the collection," Corin said, arranging mannequins outside the back door. "Not sure where they came from. They've got manufacturer's engravings on their heels, but I don't recognize the country, or city, or wherever it is."

"That's weird," the EMT replied. Every local knew what Corin did for work. "What's it say?"

"Made in Binnsend. Could be European or some place they

colonized. That doesn't narrow it down much."

"Could you let me know when you figure it out?"

"Sure," Corin said, positioning the last mannequin in the sprawling crowd. There were over thirty. Corin couldn't fit them all in the showroom. The renovated cottage serving as Corin's Wash'ashore Plastics Museum was already cramped, the original pine flooring buckling under displays and dioramas. Every wall hung heavy with debris sifted from the surf.

Once the ambulance pulled away, Corin selected the least worn mannequin and hefted it through the back door. Inside the museum, the air was cool. The cottage was built in the 1800s by his great-great-great grandfather and always felt damp.

With the mannequin cradled under his arm, Corin moved through the display section, past objects that ran aground on nearby beaches. There were yellow rubber ducks and children's pastel-blue swimming pools, Halloween masks and comic book action figures, life vests, lipstick tubes, and an entire jar of plastic tampon applicators.

The more common detritus was heaped together in aesthetically arranged piles, color coordinated in a rainbow spectrum. The countless straws and plastic soda bottles, the jellyfish-like plastic bags and cigarette filters. He had constructed a Christmas tree out of buoys and fishing line, had built a human skeleton from discarded running shoes. People came for the oddities, but the everyday objects, paired with statistics, were the real educators. The back wall was painted with a mural of the globe. Red and blue arrows traced coastlines, marking major and minor currents. Beneath he listed which carried the most plastic, which deposited the most on the ocean floor.

With his free hand, Corin opened the door to his work space. A dim computer screen cast a glow around itself. The rest of the room was left in darkness. He stood the mannequin beside his crowded desk and flipped on the overheads. The room was nothing but metal shelves of organized plastic, all labeled and cataloged. A single desk stood at its center.

Corin typed the name Binnsend into the search bar. No accurate results appeared. Pieces on raising reptiles and reconnecting with lost friends filled the screen. He altered the search, adding country names and continents, plastic plants and manufacturing hubs. Still nothing. As he pulled a world atlas from his overflowing bookcases, his door flung open.

"Can I have one?" Beth asked.

"Not yet. I need to do research first," Corin replied, dropping the atlas.

"On all of them?"

"Well, yeah. Who knows if one's different from the rest."

Beth, Corin's wife, operated an art gallery on the far edge of the property. While Corin displayed statistics and educational warnings, Beth made plastic debris into art, mostly sculptures and mosaics constructed from single-use items and bottle caps. Occasionally she carved portraits into disposable cooler foam or Styrofoam take-out containers. Her jewelry sold well. She wore a pair of crescent moon earrings cut from an old flip phone. Her blonde hair was held back by a black bandana.

"Why? Are you afraid I'll get all the foot traffic?" Beth asked, leaning against the doorframe. It was their usual joke of feigned rivalry.

Nearly three times the number of visitors passed through the art gallery's doors each summer as they did Wash'ashore Plastic. Both had door counters in their entrance ways. There was no arguing attendance. Corin didn't debate reasons one was favored over the other. He knew people liked beauty, the clean aesthetic art brought to trash. His raw, almost unfathomable data, turned viewers off. People didn't like to confront the problem they added to. People did like to buy bottle cap portraits and jellyfish statues. It funded the majority of the couples' joint venture.

"No. That's not it. If I break them up, who knows what I'll miss. The process should be easy. They've got manufacturer's marks. If you go and grind one down to make beer coasters, I could lose something," Corin said, flipping through the atlas. He ran his finger down the index at the back, searching for Binnsend. It wasn't listed amongst the B's.

"You really think one's going to be that important?" Beth asked. "I'll keep it intact and use it as a display."

"Please, just leave them where they are. I'll figure this out in a week. Two tops. After that you can take as many as you want."

"Good. There's no way you'd fit them all in here anyway," Beth said, waving a hand towards the showroom.

"You never know, people might pay to look through the windows of a cabin stuffed with mannequins."

"Very voyeuristic."

"If it gets people talking, I'd be willing to show more than just mannequins," Corin joked.

"I don't think that would further the message you're going for, Corin."

"Hey, you never know," Corin said. "People love a good spectacle for the sake of distraction."

Corin was wrong. In a week, he uncovered little information on Binnsend. After two weeks, his notes were mostly blank, the few lines scribbled down crossed out in black pen. He spent his mornings researching the mannequins. Years ago, he would have been shellfishing at such an hour, but a slipped disk in his lower back forced early retirement. In the afternoon he acted as a docent in the museum, leading tourists through his displays, lingering before the current map, explaining how plastic affects the habitats of seahorses, turtles, and other marine life.

Corin traced his finger along the line for the Gulf Stream running up the Eastern seaboard.

"The Gulf Stream deposits most of the plastic I scoop up, but the Labrador current coming down from Greenland also plays a part," Corin said.

A little kid, tucked beneath his mother's arm, raised his hand.

"What can I do for you?" Corin asked with a smile.

"What about the other arrows?" the kid asked. "Where does their trash go?"

The map had over thirty currents outlined.

"Well, the simple answer is everywhere. Even though most of our plastic is carried by two currents, you also have the South Equatorial flowing into the Caribbean, then up around Florida. But it's possible for something to be dropped into the California Current and make its way here," Corin said, indicating several arrows moving along Antarctica and up the coast of Africa.

"So this stuff could come from anywhere?" the boy asked,

pointing to the discarded shoe skeleton.

"Basically, yes. Every year eight million tons of plastic makes its way into the ocean. It comes from every continent. Most are single-use items only used for a few minutes before being thrown away," Corin said, reciting his environmental pitch. "That's why it's important we move away from using things like plastic forks or disposable coffee cups. We use them for a minute, then they clog our waters forever. Doesn't seem worth it."

The young boy nodded enthusiastically as his mother tucked a ninety-nine cent coffee behind her back.

The group of tourists thanked Corin after he answered a question about a giant plastic squid that floundered ashore from Japan, then moved off on their own, inspecting other plastic oddities. While Corin stood next to the entrance, waiting for a hoped-for follow-up, the door opened, nearly catching his shoulder. Beth burst in, dirty blond hair flowing behind her. An outrageous necklace made of braided fishing line and dulled fishing hooks clinked against one another around her neck.

"You need to look at this," she said, lassoing an arm around Corin's waist, dragging him towards the door.

"I've got visitors," he said, gesturing to the tourists.

"They're not going to steal anything," Beth replied, pulling harder.

"What if they have questions?"

Beth looked over the people standing around the glass display cases. "Does anyone have any final questions?"

A chorus of *Nopes* and *All sets* greeted her.

Corin let Beth escort him out of the room, into the early summer air. The humid season was just beginning. She led him across the grass dividing her gallery from his museum, towards the water. The two buildings sat on a clear-cut hill that dropped down to a rock strewn beach and the dock where Corin's boat was moored. It was low tide again. The smell of swamp gases and decaying marine life rose on the wind. She refused to tell him what she had seen as they walked.

"Tell me it's a mermaid," Corin said.

"Don't be a perv," Beth replied, whacking his arm.

As they drew near, Corin could see that it wasn't a mermaid, or anything else he hoped for. The bleached bodies of another twenty mannequins crowded the same sandbar as before. Their poses were different, less laid back and casual, more aggressive in their gesticulations. As Beth's sandals flapped against the dock's damp boards, he noted flexed arms and running strides half submerged in sand. They paused at the end of the dock, squinting into the sunlight reflecting in silver crescents off the waves.

"Since I found them first, I get one," Beth said.

"Fine. You're helping me move them though," Corin replied, descending into his Boston Whaler. The boat rocked under his weight.

"Why didn't these show up with the first load?" Beth asked, unfastening the mooring lines.

"There's a million possibilities. Maybe some got snagged somewhere. Maybe they fell into the ocean later. Maybe someone's messing with me. Take your pick," Corin said, starting the engine.

"Hopefully it's not the last one," Beth called over the motor. She joined him on the boat's deck, sitting on the bench spanning the middle of the fiberglass hull. Corin brought the boat to full throttle and skipped along the shallows. The water at low tide was no deeper than five feet. It took less than a minute to nose onto the bar's sandy edge.

Together they filled the boat with mannequins, fighting the muddy suck of sand while loosening their bodies from the ground. The first thing Corin did when he laid a mannequin down was check its heel. On each, he found the engraving *Made in Binnsend*.

"I want this one," Beth said, holding up a female mannequin, her hands on her hips, leaning forward as if questioning an audience.

"Works for me," Corin replied. "She's all yours."

With the last of the mannequins loaded onto the boat, Corin helped Beth settle down into a nest of plastic limbs. He pushed them off of the bar, soaking the edge of his shorts, before heading back to the dock. He'd have to add the new arrivals to the pale throng behind the museum. There wasn't much room left before they spilled around the corner, coming into view from the parking lot. He didn't want that. Didn't want questions without answers. Beth's mannequin lay across her lap. *One less I have to store*, Corin thought. He contemplated offering up more, but couldn't stand the idea of handing over a crucial subject.

Every morning, before opening Wash'ashore's doors, Corin went down to the dock to check if more mannequins washed up during the night. He thought of the trips as a way to clear his head before research. A few minutes alone in nature, the lap of waves, the flutter of birds skimming the shallows. Some days he found nothing. On others, he found entire mannequin families beached on the sand bar. Occasionally, a single white hand would emerge from the surf, but the bodies usually arrived in groups. Corin felt he was spending more time retrieving their bodies than researching them. The bulging disc in his back ached. Over the next month, he added fifty-three mannequins to the herd behind the museum. It was impossible to shield them from the public who flocked to the arrangement of barnacle-crusted models. Corin made up a sign. It looked the same as the others posted around the museum. It read *Mannequins. Unknown Origin.*

The questions he feared came in every day. He gave the same answers.

"Still haven't found the place," he'd say to tourists and locals. "Come back next week. Maybe I'll have a better idea then."

And they did come back. People visited the museum in record numbers to view the mannequins. Local news channels ran Corin's story. The papers interviewed other experts on plastics and ocean currents. None of them could offer further answers, which only brought more viewers from neighboring states.

"Maybe I shouldn't find the answer," Corin said to Beth over dinner one night.

She laughed. "That would literally annoy you until you die."

"I know. I just can't believe I haven't found anything. I've emailed college professors and librarians, map makers, and archivists. No one's heard of the place. I'm starting to think it doesn't exist."

"Or maybe they're from more than one place, you know, Frankensteined together" Beth offered, cutting into her veggie burger.

"Still doesn't explain the manufacturer's mark."

"Have you ever seen anything like this before?" Corin asked a professor from Harvard visiting the museum. He asked the same questions of everyone with a remotely scientific background: faculty from UMass, geographers from Syracuse who stepped through the museum's door, molecular engineers. *Ever heard of Binnsend? Have you ever located an unknown territory? Have you seen this mark before?*

Corin arranged the mannequins around the museum's front lawn, some in clusters, others by themselves. They looked deep in conversation, laughing over a shared joke, ranting to the sky, pleading with those around to listen. Some seemed joyous in the tilt of their spine. Others looked pained from the slant of their shoulders. Two lay on the ground, their legs eaten out from beneath them by jetty rocks or the ocean floor. Families moved through the exhibit, examining their bleached pigment. Corin left one laying on a table, heel raised so people could see the markings on the foot. *Binnsend.*

"Sounds like an old English industrial town," said a freckled woman from Oxford. "That's not it, though. Not quite. Binnend. It's missing the S. It was an old oil town that went under. Lots of refineries, but no production factories. I think it might have fallen into the sea."

The professor pointed to the region of England where the town once stood on the display map. Of course Corin had heard of the place. It came up in every search result, but the woman was the first to note it. He'd researched the town for weeks, searching for mentions of mannequin factories, or any sort of factory for that matter, inside the town. No matter how much he wanted it to be the place, there was nothing. It hadn't been misspelled.

"Did she find your town?" Beth asked after the woman and her family left.

"Close but no cigar," Corin replied.

"Sorry to hear that. How many did you add today?" Beth asked, helping Corin move a pair of muscle-bound mannequins to the edge of the display.

"Fifteen."

"How's it possible they keep showing up and no one's heard of this place?"

"Well, something is manufactured in India, stitched together in Taiwan, sent to Moldova to be dyed, then passed along to Spain for packaging. Maybe Binnsend is somewhere in between like you said, some stop we haven't heard of."

Corin imagined the sunken city of Binnend, Atlantis-like beneath the waves. Rows of barnacle-stuck factories churned out endless plastic bodies, the continual grind of cogs and gears unaffected by submergence. Waterlogged houses were plastered with seaweed and six-pack racks alike, families of crabs hunkering in eaves. Their rusting infrastructure was so congested with trash that sank from above, odd aquatic survivors sought revenge, letting their own manufactured junk float to land, to remind everyone of who they had been, the mistakes they made and continued making.

But Corin's waking dreams were rarely accurate.

Corin knew there were probably books he couldn't acquire and experts he couldn't contact on the subject. His resources had been exhausted. He'd traced everything from Nikes to life-size Dracula figurines.

Only the mannequins defied identification. Their bodies arranged along the unkempt lawn mirrored the statistics he taught on tours, their overwhelming presence a visual interpretation of the tons of plastic collecting in ocean gyres.

"It's like I said. You should never rule out a possibility," Beth added. "That's how I make art. Endless possibilities. Otherwise, you're restricted and everything becomes contrived."

"You're right," Corin replied. "I have no idea where these things come from."

"What do you think of this?" Beth asked, stepping aside from a pairing of mannequins she manipulated. They were sensually bent together, hips interlocked, pelvises brushing. Next to them, on the lawn nearby, she laid a baby mannequin, one of the more recent additions to the collection.

"Plastic begets plastic?"

"Good title. We can work with that."

"A little crass though."

"People like crass," she replied, stepping away from her work.

Corin guided his Boston Whaler on its usual route from dock to sandbar. He could see through the dissipating mist only four mannequins hung up that morning. *Thank God,* he muttered, rubbing his lower back. The day before it had been forty-three. The largest gathering yet. Some of them had been odd; extra limbs, a third arm, two heads, tails and wings, mythic appendages he could barely fathom. He piled the four relatively normal mannequins in the boat's bow. One had a stunted arm, but that was tame compared to the previous collection.

He headed the boat upwind, cutting through the surf.

Corin hauled the bodies up the slope towards the museum, which was now completely ringed by the bleached models, naked in the early morning fog. They resembled photographs of galaxies, each body a star orbiting the central hub of the building, the building few people entered anymore. They only came for the mannequins, their own likenesses reflected in the thousands, strewn about, representations of what they didn't want to acknowledge in themselves, but couldn't ignore any longer.

The mannequins were only there because people wanted to see them, wanted them to exist. They were like the other garbage people subsisted on, the tenth pair of running shoes, the seven straws to match their seven drinks at the bar, iPhone packaging. Part of Corin wondered if it was their desire that dragged the mannequins out of the ocean. Part of him still hoped there was a place on a forgotten map somewhere called Binnsend, the sunken city ever churning.

He continued to ask visitors if they heard of the country, but their answers never changed.

He was surprised to find an ambulance parked at the top of the grassy incline, idling, the lights mute. The blue uniformed EMT he had met when he first mistook the mannequins for drowning victims moved through the gathered forms. Corin figured another false alarm had brought the paramedic away from the station.

The man stopped here and there, noting arrangements, laughing at the sexual couple, the onlooker turning away from the ranting preacher.

"So did you find an answer?" the EMT asked Corin after he offloaded the newest acquisitions.

"No. I mean, if you pulled out a map, I can't point to a specific place," Corin replied.

"That's surprising."

"Yeah, I was pretty disappointed at first, but I've gotten used to the idea of not knowing."

"Well, at least they aren't in the ocean anymore."

"There's always that."

The EMT nodded, checked the radio clipped to his belt, and looked off across the field of mannequins.

"Do you mind if I look around for a bit even though you're closed?" the EMT asked.

"No worries," Corin replied. "It's not like you're disturbing anyone. Spend the day, or come back tomorrow, or the next day. I'm sure more will show up."

"Hope you don't run out of space," the EMT said, walking off through the naked bodies. He was the only dark shape among the white models, pausing momentarily to admire their design, before moving off across the hill. The edge of the group was still far off beyond the museum, bodies drifting back towards the water and the endless pull of the current and the sandbar beyond, empty for the moment.

Corin doubted that would last long.

Corey Farrenkopf lives on Cape Cod with his wife, Gabrielle, and works as a librarian. He is the fiction editor for *The Cape Cod Poetry Review*. His work has been published in or is forthcoming from *The Southwest Review, Catapult, Tiny Nightmares, Redivider, Hobart, Wigleaf, Flash Fiction Online, Bourbon Penn, Campfire Macabre*, and elsewhere. To learn more, follow him on twitter @CoreyFarrenkopf or on the web at CoreyFarrenkopf.com.

photolinguistics

Jennifer Mace

come, sit on the mountain, and
watch us speak to the stars.

their language is
morse code and phasic shifts;
we paint in roads and villages
and the hum of high-voltage
transformers, we murmur
in street lamps and stadiums
and the ill-mannered leak
of a window.

like shouting through high wind,
we are veiled
by clouds and magnetic storms and
the jealous glare of our sun

but the earth is
a glimmering bauble, and
our hands will bedeck her
with light.

Jennifer Mace is a queer Brit who roams the Pacific Northwest in search of tea and interesting plant life. A two-time Hugo-finalist podcaster for her work with *Be The Serpent*, she writes about strange magic and the cracks that form in society. Her short fiction has appeared in *Cast of Wonders* and the anthology *Skies of Wonder, Skies of Danger*, while her poetry may be found in *Liminality* and *Uncanny*. Her anthology *Silk & Steel: A Queer Speculative Adventure Anthology*, with co-editors Janine Southard and Django Wexler, may be found through Cantina Press. Find her online at www.englishmace.com.

Photo credit: Karen Osborne.

The Talking Bears of Greikengkul

Sandy Parsons

In a way, Silya had grown up with the bears. Her father had, for a time, worked for the Interspecies Language Group, cooing to the cubs and whispering dirty Slavic limericks and snippets of Tolstoy whenever the researchers left the room. He was a subversive, her mother had said, but always with a laugh. "It's why they killed him." Following the bear's lives consumed her mother and colored every facet of Silya's childhood. Each birthday since infancy Silya received a Talking Bear gift. She owned complete sets of the bean bag plushies, the coins, every trading card, including the rare Kamchatka. Her mittens frayed away from her fingers and her ribs were sharp enough to gut anyone Silya hugged, but she had Talking Bear swag out the wazoo. She could recite their individual stats, sing the ditties, and she was the first person in her class to have watched the video of the surgery where they'd been modified. It was quite boring, though, mostly shaved pink rectangles of skin among oceans of blue paper. So it surprised no one that she ended up at the university where the bears had been gifted in their retirement, and it would also have been no surprise that she snuck through the barricades between classes to hide amongst the honeysuckle and listen to them talk.

It was on one of these jaunts that Jumar found her gnawing the fence with the teeth of her pliers. There was nothing to do but let him come along. Almost immediately they found one. "Would you like a Dr. Pepper?" said the bear, standing up. The human inflection always startled Silya, but Jumar said, "Why yes," and held out his hand, even though the bear obviously was only reciting what it had heard the prior handlers say. Silya grabbed his shirt and they stumbled away, diving through the fence as the bear's claws clanged against the wire.

"You aren't supposed to engage them."
"I thought that's what you were doing."
Silya was too angry to answer. He knew the rules. She ought

to take him back to the dorm but instead she resumed her original direction. Jumar tromped after her, "You know they're going to be euthanized, don't you?"

She hadn't. "Why? That's a waste. We can learn so much from them still."

"After that student wandered into their lair, they decided it was too risky to keep them here. Besides, no one's doing any research. They're just a publicity stunt."

When she found the mother and cubs she touched a finger to his lips before he spoke. He hunkered next to her, shoulder to shoulder. The spice of him contrasted with the sweet flowers. "What is she saying?" he whispered.

She shook her head, annoyed. Didn't he understand the universal signal for shut up? But when he opened his mouth again she jutted her chin and said, "Mama, telling story to cubs."

His face scrunched into confusion as he listened. Granted it wasn't much of a story, but Silya knew the details, and she knew the particulars of the scientist who crafted it. Unlike with human fairytales, metaphor was less important than diction for the bears. Her mouth followed Mama Bear's rounding vowels and the pursing of her jowls, but the cub, still immature, mostly barked. Until it saw Silya and said her name.

No time to check if Jumar heard, she was too busy running. When they'd reached the safety of the building's interior, sliding the great bolt while tons of bear flesh pounded the outer door, he said, "Their speech is clearer than I thought it would be. But I have a question. Weren't the cubs born here?"

Silya followed the question to its logical center. "The second gen mods were genetic, allowing any cubs born with the mutation to be capable of forming words. But nobody's heard more than a roar from them as yet."

"Is that what you're looking for, why you keep going out there?" His tone was more accusing than concerned. No one had been killed by the bears in years. She shrugged, but Silya wondered, was that why? She didn't know, only that she'd been compelled to come, to listen. She thought she heard Russian from one of the older bears, once, but she couldn't be sure. When she hadn't responded Jumar said, "That cub looked right at you. I could have sworn it said your name." She felt her cheeks flush and she smiled, embarrassed but pleased. He added, "I could trap it for you."

She laughed, dropped her voice to a sexy alto. "Jumar: bear hunter." He kissed her and they didn't talk about it anymore.

Silya was too busy with classes over the next few weeks to visit the bears or Jumar's dorm. Greikengkul University got a lot of students on its bear gimmick, but it was as tough a slog as any university. She was awakened from a nap by the *Kodiak Cantata*, her mother's ringtone. When she answered, peeling Sociology notes from her sweaty forehead, her mother said, "Don't babble, Misia." Silya's wide yawn had her imagining herself one of the bears. Her mother's next words snapped her to fully woke human. "It's all over the news. Some poor fool has gotten trapped by the bears. Do you know who it is?"

A certain poor fool had been joking, surely. She typed in the link her mother recited. The news cameras only showed the outside of the largest cave, restless bears pacing, pawing the air and grumbling about the dean. The Greikengkul representative was belaboring that this was the dean of the former owner's college, and that the bears were quite content in their new environment. Silya's mother said, "Oh that looks like Penny. Her red ruff is getting some grey. Just like me. I miss them. I wish the . . . ."

"I'm going to go check it out. I'll call you back when I know more."

"Make sure they don't hurt the poor darlings. Send me pictures."

It was warm out, but Silya layered on a nylon undershirt, sweater and jacket, stuffed gloves and hat in her pocket. At the last second she pocketed her roommate's pepper spray. As she followed the trail grooved by her many trips to the hidden entry spot, she called Jumar. No answer. She swiped her phone to leave a message, a noncommittal, *hey, where are you*, but Jumar had sent her one instead. *I'm coming by tonight with a surprise.*

That was confirmation enough who the poor fool was, and she altered her course, now moving along the electric fence until the wiry arms stretched over the river. The narrow gap between wire and concrete might deter a bear, but a person could squeeze through. She'd then have to figure how to climb the embankment or swim upstream, salmon-like. Which called to mind a memory. She and her mother laughing as the bears stood in the middle of a salmon run. One was saying *hey watch this*, but the altered mouth was suddenly filled with a fish. The other bears made a sound, something like a bark or a sneeze and her mother had told her that was bear laughter.

A growl interrupted Silya's thoughts and she lost her balance. Theodore, her mother's least favorite, who only spoke when a treat was involved, at the top of the hill. He didn't speak now, which she found encouraging. The action of turning caused her to lose her traction on the slick concrete and she slid on her butt and soles into a stream of leaves and bear shit. Theodore blew a strawberry of dismissal and sauntered off. Dank rotting leaves coated her sneakers and the acid feral smell of urine made her eyes burn. Did the bears mark the entrance or was this some other animal? She thought again of her mother, who never ascribed anything but human attributes to the talking bears. She would have claimed they were above shitting in the woods, much less marking their territory, even as she changed the diaper of what was left of Silya's father.

Google maps showed the bear's main cave system was several kilometers to the west, but Silya knew of another entrance. Modern lore among the students, for it was where the remains of the golden-haired girl had been discovered. If you knew what to look for, a path once used by a drug cartel led to the hidden entrance. A pattern of stones, a shadow from the mountain at a particular hour.

She pushed aside branches and a coarse thatch of brush. Once inside she heard her name echoing through the tunnel. "Jumar," she called, and was answered by a growl. A tawny cub appeared. It opened its maw sideways, ferocious and adorable at the same time. She didn't recognize this as one of the talking bears, although her mother would have known. "Do you speak?"

The bear shook its head, an action that might have been comical if it didn't then charge her and clamp down on her forearm. Through Silya's terror she heard her name bouncing off the walls, low, watery, urgent, mingling with her cry of pain. The cub jerked its head, tearing through leather and cloth, but leaving her with only a superficial wound.

"Silya." From behind her, louder now. She turned to find a

woman, the warden, who held a gun pointed in the direction of the departing bear. She turned the gun on Silya. "Are you Silya?"

"Yes."

"Come with me."

Silya followed the woman out of the cave, and the whispers of her name amongst other murmurs followed them. As they walked toward a jeep with two more wardens, Silya noticed the muzzles of the guns aimed at her. "Am I under arrest?"

"Why are you on a first name basis with these bears?" the first warden asked as she helped Silya into the jeep and spread apart the edges of her wounded jacket. The other wardens leaned in, nodding, the brims of their hats tapping.

"Have you found Jumar...I mean, have you rescued the person trapped by the bears?"

A warden cleaned her arm, wrapped it. "Not yet. Can you really converse with them? We were told they only mimic speech."

"I have spoken to them before," she admitted. In normal circumstances the admission would get her kicked out of the university. "They never answered intelligibly. But I will try again."

The wardens offered her a helmet with a mask. The grill cage looked too much like fangs, so she refused. "You'll be with me, so I won't need it," Silya explained, pointing at the woman's gun. The puppet lines of the warden's mouth deepened but she waved Silya to stay close to her as they entered the main cave. A man with a microphone was saying to a camera, "The number one threat—" Flashes and shouts drowned out the rest, but as soon as Silya and the warden were inside, a stench of rotting fruit and ursine urine made smell the primary sense, so that sound no longer mattered. Jumar's shredded backpack taunted them. They stepped around the strewn contents, Bit-O-Honey wrappers, keys and an orange inhaler, and moved into darkness. *Huff-huff* noises bounced at them.

The warden held the rifle in one hand and put the other on Silya's arm. She whispered in a knowledgeable tone, "They make that sound to warn you off."

Pulling away and feeling along the mossy, clammy stones,

Silya spoke to the darkness. "Do you know me?"

A pale snout, the ancient scars x-ed along it into a grotesque smile, entered the faint circle of light. This was Alana, or perhaps Dorie, from the first generation. The bear said, "Do you know the song of Silya?"

"Yes. Would you like me to sing it?"

The bear took another step. "The doctor will see you now."

Silya sensed the warden behind her, raising the gun. She said to Alana or Dorie, "I'd like to see Jumar. Is he okay?"

"Trust me, this won't hurt you."

"I know that." Silya decided to take the bear's offer at face value and raised her foot, as if she might step around the bear. A metal clicking behind her made the bear look up. It showed bloodied teeth. "Is Jumar in there?"

The bear laughed. The sound was not the sneezing her mother had described but it wasn't an imitation of the researcher's either. It was a new sound, and yet a clear sound of amusement.

The bear lunged. The warden's rifle was quicker and the bear fell. With her ears ringing Silya asked, "Did you kill her?"

"Only stunned, but if I have to shoot her again, the dose would be lethal. Hurry." Silya felt along the cold wall, stepping from moss to something slick and crunchy. Bones. "Jumar?" Silence. Silya moved fast, letting her palm on damp stone be a guide.

She started to sing, "Little bear little bear, are you alone there?" Her voice cracked and she swallowed hard. "I'm sending my daughter to visit your lair. Silya, we call her—"

Silya. Silya. Silya. Sibilance echoed all around, drowning out her voice. Silya's eyes had grown accustomed to the dark but the warden was no longer behind her, had not been for some time now.

Jumar's body leaned against the stone wall. His smiling eyes didn't seem to notice the rest of his face had been chewed off. From behind her a bear said, "No words in there. We checked the Wernicke's." It laughed, that new talking bear chortle, and was joined by others. They moved around her, sniffing, some of them humming like her father had. A cub rolled back and forth, holding its feet. "Silya," it said, "do you know how the song of Silya ends?"

For an instant Silya was at a loss for words. The bears had always spoken in sentences that mimicked the researchers who had worked with them; this was the first time one had spoken an independently intelligent question. Communication was the key. If she could teach the bears to speak they could speak for themselves and make their own case for a place in the world. The bears herded her closer to the fire, into its light, where words from flesh became meaning.

Sandy writes literary, philosophical, humorous, and speculative fiction. She has studied physics, math, molecular biophysics, and medical science, but only ponders the fundamental nature of reality for fun these days. When not writing, Sandy works as an anesthetist in Georgia and is an associate editor at *Escape Pod*. More information and a list of publications can be found at https://www.sandyparsons.com/.

We Have So Little Time Left

D. Dina Friedman

Already, the sunlight is shrinking like an old shirt
that barely covers the belly, even while it glows
gilding the dried up cattails, the snapped branches
that pierce the cloudless sky like a severed bone.

Only smudges of light left on the slick leaves
languishing in icy mud, and on the rushing squirrels,
newly fattened for their long, incredible fast.
Fewer acorns endure under the detritus

to trip our balance. The sky is less blue,
the slippery light distant, when it isn't daring us
with glare. All the garden vegetables remaining
taste like old, cold dirt.

Soon my jaw will forget how to release from its clench
against the elements, and soon we'll crave the elements,
predictable days of final growth—the hardening
stems racing to ripen before turning to rot.

The air will sizzle, and some far away bed
of ice will implode, or simply drip. Death
by a thousand small cuts. But tonight, like every night,
the sun will set in its predictable pattern, cutting off

another sliver of our lives. And we might crawl
into bed with a cup of tea, a fantasy
story while fat squirrels scutter up snags
of what once upon a time were trees.

D. Dina Friedman has published fiction and poetry in many literary journals (including *The Sun, Aji, Cider Press Review, Hawaii Pacific Review, Lilith, Negative Capability, Rhino, Common Ground Review, Crab Orchard Review, Steam Ticket, New Plains Review, Blue Stem,* and *Anderbo)* and received two Pushcart Prize nominations for poetry and fiction. She is the author of two YA novels, *Escaping Into the Night* (Simon and Schuster) and *Playing Dad's Song* (Farrar Straus Giroux) and one chapbook of poetry, *Wolf in the Suitcase* (Finishing Line Press). Dina is also a political activist focusing on immigration and racial justice issues, which often find their way into her writing. Originally from New York City, Dina now lives in western Massachusetts next door to a farm with 500 cows. Dina has an MFA from Lesley University and teaches at the University of Massachusetts/Amherst. Visit her website at http://www.ddinafriedman.com.

Mummies

Steve Rasnic Tem

"The Egyptians understood the rise of the sun each day was not guaranteed."

"Please pause." The house voice stopped. Dev missed the kind female persona almost instantly, but he needed focus. He owned a dozen books on ancient Egypt and wanted to donate some or all. He didn't require any of them since he had digital copies. Physical books could be a deceptive comfort. Sometimes he forgot owning the knowledge was not the same as possessing it.

He'd planned to spend his retirement making a path through world history. That plan, like so many others, died with Emily. Ten years later, and he'd given no thought to history until the past few months, when the mountains began burning again.

Farnaby was barking. He'd just let him out, and there was plenty of shade, but he'd best get him soon. Outside on an August afternoon wasn't a safe place for either small dogs or old men.

Tomorrow morning he'd take him for a ride into the foothills if the heat, smoke, and ash permitted. He didn't know what dogs needed; Farnaby was his first since childhood. But Dev needed out of the house. He wanted to see if the city was still something like what he remembered.

"Please read the part about what I might find in an ancient Egyptian garbage dump." He couldn't help himself. Questions popped into his head, and if he didn't ask them immediately, he was likely to forget.

The woman's voice continued. "At Oxyrhynchus archaeologists found hundreds of thousands of bits of papyrus including unknown Sappho poems, plays, and the lost Gospel of Thomas. Other dump sites have provided bits of pottery, tools, religious artifacts, as well as thousands of limestone flakes bearing the practice writing of scribes, daily entries, love notes, complaints, and other texts of historical interest."

"So, one's man's treasure," Dev said. She didn't answer.

His late friend Lyle should have had a dog. A dog might have saved him, but Dev hadn't understood that five years ago. Lyle was a major reason Dev was reducing his footprint, leaving less for his daughter to sort out after he was gone.

He never went inside the house when he picked up Lyle, but he saw the curtains snug against the windows from the press of accumulation, the random junk sitting in the side yard, the trash spilling from under a garage door that wouldn't close all the way. He knew very well what must have been going on inside Lyle's home. The police found Lyle entombed in his bedroom wrapped in his belongings, in a house without power or running water.

Dev used the Egyptian books to fill one of the Donate boxes and emptied three shelves of fiction into several others. He stacked these into the corner along with several bags of clothing, sacks full of household items he would never use, and a crate of small electronics most of whose function now escaped him. There were still thousands of items in his home. He knew appropriate decisions on most of these would require some sort of breakthrough, a change in perspective that would turn their presence from comforting to annoying.

"Please continue."

"The Egyptians spent significant time and resources preparing for their deaths, filling their tombs with items needed for the journey. The afterlife was their future, their science fiction, and every day it rubbed through into their now."

There was more, but he gradually came to acknowledge the commotion erupting outside. Farnaby. He'd only let the Scottish Terrier out to relieve himself. "Please, what's the current temperature?"

"One Hundred Thirty Degrees Fahrenheit." Dev rushed to the door and slammed it open into a blast of heat, reached behind to close it and keep the cool air inside, and inadvertently grabbed the hot handle.

He may have screamed, he wasn't sure. He bent over in agony, shaking his burnt fingers, sucking in the smoke-flavored air. Everything looked a smoldering yellow. Farnaby barked excitedly, both at Dev's trembling fingers and the new thing clinging to the Maple tree.

The creature stuck to the tree was hard to distinguish from the bark, being little more than a subtle shift in the pattern. Some insect he had never seen before, three or four inches long, twig-like with a triangular head. Some sort of mantis perhaps. They'd lost the crickets for good. So, was this their replacement?

"Farnaby! Come!" He stumbled to the door and grabbed the handle with his shirttail, letting the dog precede him, and once inside struggled up the stairs and got his hand under a cool stream of water. He could hear the soft murmur of the Please voice downstairs. He hadn't ordered it off, and it still prattled on to an empty room about dead Egyptians and their adventures in a highly anticipated afterlife.

"The first rulers of Egypt were ancient even to the Romans. Cleopatra lived closer to the invention of the self-driving automobile than she did to the building of the Great Pyramid." At this distance she sounded like a whisper in his ear, but that small bit of perspective still impressed. "Please stop." His voice was hoarse, but she obeyed.

He stared out the window at the burning mountains, disappeared beneath a deep mustard-colored veil. Dev realized somewhere beneath all that accumulating ash lay his Emily's ashes. He couldn't decide if this should horrify or comfort him.

He tried to see through the smoke, looking for any bit of remembered detail. His view rapidly deteriorated.

Part of the reason he and Emily bought this place was because of the view, and the mature landscaping that came with it. Forty-two different flowering plants at that time, blossoms staggered through the seasons. He used to take photos of flower buds breaking into bloom, of insects crawling over petals and stems, jewels of dew suspended in early morning webs, a world often unnoticed, and delicate as a dream.

The growing seasons for a number of those plants had since shifted by months. Many died because he couldn't water them enough, and some no longer survived in Colorado's climate. Was this the future invading his now?

When his hand felt better, he dried it gingerly, applying lotion and a loose bandage. Farnaby gazed at his wrappings mournfully.

"So, I'm part mummy now, kiddo."

He couldn't find anything identical to the new bug on the web. The closest was a smaller Bark Mantis from Honduras. It was far north of its usual territory, but habitats and migration ranges had been evolving for years.

He resisted the impulse to ask the house to read to him some more. As comforting as it was to hear another voice, he had other things to think about. He seldom asked for the news. He had no need for daily updates on what fresh hell waited for him outside.

He picked up a book, *The Next Hundred Years*, thoroughly worn from reading. He'd owned it a good twenty years. There were few things more useless than an old book of predictions. It fell open to the chapter "Upload Yourself," this exploration of a future world in which dying folk could upload their minds to a computer network to escape death, living out eternity in this oh-so-vivid ultra hi def afterlife modeled from their own specifications. But what right did anyone have to escape into an eternity where the sky was always blue and nature this sensuous intoxication when the world you left behind was in flames?

The doorbell rang and the living room screen lit up with an image of the grocery delivery man in his dazzling reflective suit. Farnaby raced to the door barking frantically. Dev watched the screen until the man left his porch. He opened the door and hollered "Thank you!" as he gathered up the bags. The man turned and waved and returned a "You're welcome!" Such a banal exchange, but many weeks this was Dev's only in-person human interaction.

With frequent price spikes and shortages Dev had to study the choices carefully to see what he could afford. Some months he spent nearly forty percent of his income on food, pre-World War One levels. It didn't bother him Farnaby's food cost more than his own, but it was something he couldn't tell his daughter.

He always went to bed early. Electricity was available for certain hours of the day, and for most nights not at all without a permit.

"In the Victorian era mummy unwrapping was a social event. Mummies were in plentiful supply and you could buy one for your parlor if you so desired. Mummies were burned like coal on some rail lines, ground up and made into medicines or paint, their wrappings used to make paper."

Early the next morning they got into the car and Dev told it where he wanted to go, and the approximate timing required for Farnaby's bathroom breaks. He could request a change in route at any time during the trip, but the car wouldn't permit him to go anywhere he wasn't allowed, or which might put them in danger from fire, flood, or other hazards. It knew far more about the projected weather, road conditions, and traffic patterns than he did so he was content to let the car do its job. Not that he had much choice. Dev was no longer licensed to use the manual override.

Farnaby huddled in the seat against him, head up and mouth pulled back in a rictus grin. This wasn't one of the newer SDEVs, but it featured full length transparent doors on both sides for optimal viewing, superior climate control, and enhanced air filtration. Owning such a vehicle for limited use was the only extravagance Dev permitted himself.

Within a few miles of his neighborhood they were surrounded by crumbling concrete ribbons of highway, abandoned buildings of rusting steel and coarse cement, and much more traffic than he'd anticipated. Half the lanes were devoted to large electric commuter buses spaced breathtakingly close. This was supposed to be safe, but Dev could barely stand to watch them. Farnaby had his muzzle pressed against the door, apparently fascinated by these vehicles he'd never seen before. Dev heard new work schedules started early because of the heat and ended after dark for a workweek of three days, but he hadn't paid much attention to such concerns since retirement.

Traffic in the recreational lanes was relatively light, so they were making good progress until Farnaby suddenly made whimpering sounds and began bobbing his head. "Please, we need a bathroom break," Dev announced.

"Leaving the highway." The voice was off-key and grating. It had been that way for a while, but Dev didn't consider it worth fixing.

As they exited onto a local street Dev saw a tattered scarecrow of a man standing on the corner holding a blank cardboard sign. He wore an older style reflective suit ripped in several places, the trousers coming apart at the seams and mended with tape and pieces of dirty canvas or cloth. The floppy, broad-brimmed hat pulled down around his head did not disguise his wide-eyed gaze. The portions of his arms peeking through the rips were burnt and raw looking.

As they made the turn the man jumped up and down and pointed at his sign. He shouted something, but Dev couldn't make out any specific words.

Desperate, unhinged behavior was not uncommon in people living on the ragged edge. Dev wondered if the man had a shelter to go to as the day wore on and the temperature rose. Someday he wanted to talk to someone like this, find out what their life was like, but he was ashamed to admit he was too afraid.

He wasn't alone in this. People feared each other. You could no longer trust the sky over your head or the ground beneath your feet.

The car pulled over by an empty lot amid shuttered and decaying buildings. A faded sign proclaimed *Springs' Reclamation Garden: Victory Over Climate Change*. These had been popular twenty years ago, trucking in topsoil to cover ruined spaces and create something rich with green. Although there were pale vines and anemic flowers, scattered patches of weeds, most of the lot was barren.

A few crows explored the ground. Songbirds had almost disappeared, but crows were thriving. It wasn't their fault, and there wasn't enough time to grieve over every single thing the world had lost, but Dev still resented their presence.

The car doors began to open, then shut again as a sudden cloudburst washed that view away. Farnaby looked anxious but waited patiently. They seldom received an enduring rain, just these overly dramatic explosions of thunder, shadow, and downpour lasting a few minutes or less. Soon Dev was standing in the brown grass at the edge of the lot, watching the terrier nosing around the sad-looking piece of ground.

"Stay close," he said, as if the dog understood him. But that's what you did with dogs, wasn't it? He wasn't afraid of him running away, but maybe of someone snatching him—that would be awful. He didn't want him getting into things, getting stung or tick infested. Ticks didn't die in the winter anymore. They drove Farnaby crazy all year long.

Something shiny and red in the ground caught his eye. It was curved and protruded a half inch or so above the dirt alongside a flattened clump of vegetation. He glanced around and saw other red bits, blue bits, portions of drinking cups, paper and plastic trash, a long line of rusted metal. Trash was rising out of the earth after the hard rain.

He got Farnaby into the vehicle and they headed back toward

the highway. He didn't see the tattered man anywhere. Dev hoped he'd found a safe spot to shelter before the day heated up. But it was unlikely to be a place with air conditioning. AC had become the crucial dividing line between the haves and have nots. Many could not afford it, and that meant death for some. People could get a medical subsidy if they qualified, but those qualifications became stricter every year.

It wasn't that people didn't care, and most understood their responsibility, recycling everything possible, using clean energy and conserving water. Yet the oceans continued to rise due to the damage already done, the ice caps and glaciers continued to disappear. The arctic was ice-free year-round. The indigenous population had largely left, although some attempted to stay close to home, working for the big shipping operations and oil companies. Maybe it wasn't the kind of work they should have been doing, but how could you blame them?

As the car climbed the foothills they passed through a bluish fog and then a yellow one, and then into a relatively clear band of air between the fog and the smoke across the mountains above. As the day heated up the fog would burn away and the smoke would drop lower to obscure everything, but they would be back home by then.

The car pulled off to the side. "This is the highest you may go. Waiting for further instructions."

Dev was disappointed. He'd been sure they could go higher. "Open doors please." They got out but Farnaby refused to leave his side. He kept staring at the distant brush, the shadows beneath the trees. Dev couldn't see anything, but he knew animals were coming out of the mountains to escape the wildfires looking for food, water, and shelter. He had no intention of staying outside the car for long.

He couldn't say the view had been worth the trip. The nearby trees were yellow and brittle even during summer. A few still had moss, but it was faded. Both further up the hillside and in the distance, he saw long stretches of dead trees like painted gray stripes in the canopy. He remembered a pond with waterfowl, blackbirds, the occasional fox. He wasn't sure, but he could see a dark patch of ground with a few dead cat o' nine tails which might once have been that beautiful sanctuary.

When Kelly was small, he and Emily would show her what the city looked like from this higher, calmer perspective. Not only could he not see the city today, the air smelled like garbage.

Dev wouldn't claim to be a great outdoorsman. He'd never enjoyed camping, preferring a comfortable bed in an air-conditioned hotel room. But he always knew how lucky they were to live in a state with such wonders. As Kelly grew older every summer he and Emily took her to some beautiful Colorado setting for an extended stay. Emily set up a scrapbook, and Kelly filled it with postcards and photos, pressed flowers, leaves, brochures, and her little notes about what she witnessed on these trips. He should have given the scrapbook to Kelly a long time ago, but he wasn't quite ready to let it go.

He recalled Maroon Bells, with its two purple-and-white-striped peaks mirrored in an alpine lake. It was still there, he'd heard, but difficult to get to with the heat and the fires. The road was closed most years.

They'd spent two weeks at the Great Sand Dunes, where Medano Creek emerged every spring from the Sangre de Cristos behind the dunes to form an oasis, to disappear late August for another year. It was now dried up and apparently gone forever.

Hanging Lake, though, had been her favorite. They made three trips to see this magical body of water clinging to the edge of the mountain, multiple waterfalls cascading off moss-covered stone into the still pool below. She was grown when it was destroyed by a massive forest fire that consumed most of the mountain, the site disintegrating in the resulting landslide and erosion. She'd called him, sobbing, to tell him the news.

Dev had lost all desire to travel. It wasn't just an issue of his age or his stamina. He was afraid there was no place he could go on this ailing planet and not see more signs of its demise. He felt powerless about many things, but especially in the face of climate, a system so vast it overlapped both thousands of miles of land and sea and generations of time. It was impossible for one person to engage a phenomenon so immense. But at least people should be encouraged to open their mouths and speak the truth of their grief.

When they got home the landline was flashing and a soft but persistent alarm emanated from his screen. He'd never seen this before and his first thought was there'd been an evacuation warning. "Please answer!" he cried, louder than intended, and sank into a chair. Farnaby crawled under the antique coffee table.

Kelly filled the frame, larger than life-size. He regretted

getting one so big. Like everyone else in the world he'd watched the terrible final months of coastal Bangladesh as it disappeared into the ocean, the human tragedy playing out live and magnified in his living room.

"Dad, where were you? I've been checking the cameras for hours." She was calling from the hospital, still in her mask and gown. She was a small woman, his precious child, and his first thought was she looked cute in her surgical gear, but of course he didn't say that.

"I'm sorry. Farnaby and I drove into the foothills. I guess I should have let you know I was leaving."

"No, no, I'm not your keeper. I just got really worried. This heat wave, and the air is so bad. I checked the cameras in every room, even the bathroom. Sorry. There are a few blind spots in the system. I was afraid you were lying dead in one of them."

Dev hadn't known there were blind spots. He made a mental note. They'd installed it two years ago; a camera system so emergency services and nervous adult children could check up on their elderly parents. There were tiny cameras with sensors in one corner of the ceiling of every room. He'd pretty much forgotten about them.

"Well, I'm okay. I see you're at work."

She pulled her mask down. "It's been a busy day. Too many respiratory cases to keep up. Is *your* breathing okay?"

"I'm fine, honey. Really."

"I saw all those boxes and bags. Are you getting rid of more stuff?"

"Trying to. Sometimes it's hard to let go of things."

"You know I worry when you do that. I'm always afraid you're giving up."

"Not giving up at all. Just focusing, creating space in my home, and by extension creating space in my head."

Farnaby came out from under the table then, staring at the screen, head cocked to one side.

"Hi Farnaby!" He sat up, tail wagging. "You know I still can't believe you got a dog. I told you to get one after Mom died but you were adamant you didn't want one."

"At that time, I couldn't handle being responsible for another life. I didn't even want plants in the house."

"He's so small and chipper! I figured you'd want a big old

hound with a sad face and droopy ears."

"I would never own a pet who looked like me."

"Oh Dad—"

"He keeps me company. But some days I can't get a word in edgewise."

"But that name? It's cute, but how'd you come up with that?"

"It's the main character from Aldous Huxley's final novel *Island*. It's about a utopia."

"Do you believe in that stuff? Utopias?"

"Not really. The problem with utopians is every time you turn around, they're trying to kill people."

"It was a modest afterlife for the common folk, marginally better than their lives before, but dead pharaohs might dwell among the stars at the end of their journey. The royals, the wealthy and educated could afford a tomb or coffin decorated with inscriptions providing food and magic spells to foil the demons and fiery lakes encountered. As final insurance, your family could arrange for a scarab placed within the mummy wrappings above your heart, inscribed with a spell which magically hid all your wrongdoing from final judgement."

If you had enough wealth and knowledge, you could get away with almost anything. Some things hadn't changed in 2,500 years.

Dev spent part of every day wrapped in expensive filtered and conditioned air, peeking through his front windows at his local neighborhood, a narrow view between heavy curtains. He understood how lucky he was, how privileged, with guaranteed retirement income and a daughter devoted to his well-being. He wasn't a rich man, but his imagined needs had never been too large for his revenue. As far as that wild man he saw yesterday was concerned, Dev indeed dwelled among the stars.

If he didn't see a neighbor for an extended period he wondered if they'd died or moved to a location more bearable. You rarely saw someone die. One day you noticed they were gone. It was like what happened to the missing plants and bugs, the songbirds, the coral reefs.

The suicide rate was quite high. Very few of those happened in public. Sometimes it seemed a miracle to be able to live at all. Dev didn't fear dying, but he lived every day anticipating an end: of some species, some comforting ritual, some cherished location.

He hadn't told Kelly this, but many days he felt too tired to get out of bed, or to climb out of a chair, or to choose. Did the cameras see his fatigue? Each day he waited for the exhaustion to pass, knowing someday it would not.

He saw the men walking up to his porch with their wagon. They were dressed similarly to the fellow from yesterday, with bits of reflective suit, wide floppy hats, dirty surgical masks, and pieces of homemade patchwork consisting of netting, disintegrating padding, cardboard, metal, and reflective tape. This ragged outfit had become a kind of uniform for those who wandered or attempted to live outside. His neighborhood, being so close to major routes, had frequent wanderers.

He waited as the older one walked onto the porch and rang the bell. On the screen his face around the mask looked stiff and leathery, shriveled, and expressionless. The younger man remained at the bottom of the steps guarding the wagon. Dev checked the other camera views. There was no one else in sight. On the second ring Dev spoke. "Can I help you?"

The older man paused for a moment, then turned his dark eyes toward the camera over the door. "Anything, please?" The young man said something, and the old man said something back. "Anything you can spare?"

Dev thought the accent was different from the Mexican Spanish he was used to. When the two men talked their speech was full of slang. He didn't understand a word. Honduran, maybe? Like the newly arrived Mantis in his backyard. Like much of Central America, Honduras was burning down. When your house was burning down, you left it.

"Wait just a second. Oh, do you like books?"

The old man blinked. His eyes looked enormous above the mask. "I like to read."

Dev went downstairs and retrieved one of the books on Egypt, and at the last second snagged a volume of Neruda off a shelf. He brought them upstairs and opened the hall closet. Stacked inside were boxes full of food, medicine, odd items like gloves, flashlight, batteries, a little cash. He slipped the books into the box on top and carried it to the door. "I'm terribly sorry, but please step off the porch and wait." He was embarrassed every one of the many times he'd said this, but he was a cautious man.

Dev watched the screen as the man went back down the steps and joined his partner. Then he stepped out onto the porch into the fuggy air and set the box down. He smiled at them apologetically. "Please take these. I hope they help you on your journey." He wanted to say more. He wanted to ask the elderly man what it was like to be old where he came from, to be old and wandering now through this darkening and unforgiving place. But he did not, could not, and went back inside.

He watched them on the screen as they loaded the box into their wagon and left, then switched cameras to follow their slow progress down the street, to the next house, and the one after.

The air became grainier as additional smoke settled in. More shambling figures joined them, some with wagons, some with dogs.

Whatever future there might be was manifesting here, right now, rubbing its way into the present. Dev turned away and went around checking windows, securing doors, closing himself in for the night.

A Colorado resident, Steve Rasnic Tem is, according to Joe Lansdale, "a school of writing unto himself." Steve is a past winner of the World Fantasy, British Fantasy, and Bram Stoker Awards (including 2014's Blood Kin for novel). He has published over 450 short stories in a 40+ year career. You'll find some of his best in *Figures Unseen: Selected Stories*. His latest is *The Night Doctor* and *Other Tales from Centipede Press*. He's done volunteer work for various climate change groups including 2020 or Bust and Citizens' Climate Lobby.

The Drought

All We Have Left Is Ourselves

Oyedotun Damilola Muees

The long list of blame is endless. We point fingers at each other. Someone says Adam caused it. *Why did he allow Eve to deceive him?* The women point the fingers right back at the men. *You should be ashamed of yourselves. Real men take responsibility for their actions.* The juju man blames no one in particular. *Our ancestors are infuriated at us. We have bitten more than we can chew.* The pastors and Imams are not left out in the paroxysm. *We need to atone for our sins. The Redeemer is coming soon. Rapture is at hand.* There is the man who is making money from the scourge. He puts up a charade. *The government has failed us. Where are the palliatives for the down-trodden and low income earners?* The scientist blames it on dwellers of earth. We all. *Mother Earth is currently an oblate spheroid. Your actions made her this way.* A small group who want to save the environment from pulverization gather to educate the people, telling them to do their part. *Protect your environment. The environment is a sentient being. She will fight back if abused.*

Bunch of hypocrites. You want my opinion on the current happenings? We are the ones who stuff heaps of garbage on the culvert, waiting for the waste truck to come dispose of it. And when we don't see them, we pray for the rain to come, tossing all our trash in the undulating flow. I see the juju man's signature: the blood of the dead chicken on the three-road junction. The lifeless chicken, rotting on the road until the sun dries what is left of it. The opulent man is also guilty. He rubs his wealth on us all, building a mansion that extends, blocking the channel of water. The government appeals to the *landlady* of the sea, appeasing her with sacrifice. They build exorbitant houses after sand-filling the beach—Oceanview Estate they call it. The harmless little children, too. Taking a heavy dump in the canal. Dysentery, cholera, malaria: pervasive in our locality like the vast blue sky. How will I forget the company that is the crux of this problem. Plant-17. The gigantic establishment that posed as the messiah. They give us a transformer, and in turn hijack our sight. They offer us food and later infect our farms with toxic residue of their product. They offer us jobs, and we spend the emolument on hospital bills. They furnish our schools, sensitize our children to the danger of not protecting the environment. Little did we know that we gave the devil a room in our domicile. Now he has chosen not to leave, inviting his associates. All we want is to survive. No matter what it takes. Mother Earth is on a vacation somewhere on a beach in Hawaii. Perhaps in Obudu Cattle Ranch, sipping on coconut drink and basking in the comfort of a masseur.

Do you still want my opinion on the current happenings? I suggest you grab an N95 mask, soldier boots, and your camera, and follow me. Because out there is fucking jungle, eat or get eaten.

It begins with a tocsin. We wake up from the deep sleep, thinking the long awaited rapture has finally arrived. This is not rapture—that is, if rapture has not already taken place. Everyone wakes up with that agility instilled by a clarion call. The bugle sound shoots through our ears again. Yolanda is still covered in her duvet. I nudge her. 'Yoli. Yoli. Wake up. The buyers are here,' I say, knotting the lace of my boot. She doesn't say anything. I pull the duvet off her half-naked body. I see her sallow eyes. She coughs, a dry one. Not again. Yolanda's cough has been persistent, going on for weeks. At the incipient stage we thought it was triggered by the coconut and palm kernel nuts she eats on a regular. But it is not that. It is something more baleful. I cup Yolanda's jaw in my hand, checking her eyes as if I could diagnose the problem. Later, I run off with my *Ghana-must-go* bag to meet the others.

You see, everyone living in Ajeshima is a scavenger. Stealing is highly prohibited. Whoever you were before this wave doesn't matter. If you want to pay your rent, eat some not-too-healthy food, and smoke good weed, you have to sell something. A group of elite came to our aid two months back. The largess they brought sustained us for a while, until we were all out. Then the situation changed. They asked for something in return. Now we fan out to where we can find goods, garner whatever we can; iron scraps, used cans, nuts and bolts, plastic, anything worthy of an exchange. This group gives us boots, N95 and gas masks. You get paid by the measure of your hunt—bottled water, food stuff, and medical assistance. Payment in cash is small except if what you are selling is huge.

After the trade, I approach the man in charge, telling him of Yolanda. Her incessant croak cough. He thinks it is a minor sickness. I beg him to wait while I bring Yolanda to him. 'It will cost you. Time is expensive these days,' he says, winking at me. He wants me to fuck him. No way! I have a full sack of used cans that can cover Yolanda's bills.

'Go fuck yourself,' I tell him. He turns back, heads into the chopper.

Back in the hostel, Yolanda is still sleeping. Her cough aggravates. People in the camp are muttering. I hope she doesn't have the flu. There is a law sacrosanct to all. Anyone who has the flu gets temporarily evicted until management thinks the person is better enough to return.

Austin comes to her aid. He was a 500-level undergraduate of Medicine and Surgery before all of this. He is the closest thing to a doctor in the hostel. Austin covers his nose with an N95 and rubber gloves. Yolanda does as she is told. *Widen your eyes. Open your mouth. Cough once. Twice.* He asks her some questions, too. Taking notes.

He beckons me outside. This cannot be good. 'She has asbestosis,' he says. 'The antibiotics we have here cannot do the magic. She will be needing something stronger.'

Yolanda asks what the problem is. It is her health. She has the right to know. The reaction on her face is far from what I expected. It is gaiety. I know that frame on her face. She thinks it is time for her to go meet her maker.

'We will get through this. I assure you,' I say, locking her hand in mine.

Footsteps approach behind me. All of them wearing protective kits. They have come for Yolanda. Austin must have told them about her sickness. I do not blame him. He risks getting evicted to the wetland if he doesn't report a sickness that may be noxious to the populace. Yolanda calls out to me, acting contumacious.

'Please don't let them take me away.' She fights back.

My hands are tied. There is nothing I can do. I want her to get better even if it means going away for a while. I am pissed at many things. An avalanche of rage bobs in my head. I head over to the area where we take a shit. A boy with a ringworm-streaked head walks past me. He is only wearing a colorless pant with holes. Buzzing flies trail his bum. I squat, doing my *business.* Plopping sound, *bdum bdum,* drops in the blackwater below the shack. Yolanda is the only person close to a family I have. How can I go on living if she dies? The rage blistering my heart has exacerbated. I don't take cognizance of the pervert boys watching me from the door hole until someone asks what they're doing there.

I have always had a penchant for photography. Taking pictures of nature, wildlife, that sort of it. I saw an advert for interns at a company. After pitching them my idea, they suggested I send them my best shots. Tolu, my friend, suggested I bring them pictures of rural areas. People like crude pictures. The search began, until I landed in Ajeshima. *What a perfect place for a shot,* I thought. Ajeshima is at the boundary of two local governments. You cannot be oblivious of the berm, the vast river meandering through a large body flanked by overgrown bushes, boys wearing dreadlock sitting in a canoe rolling dried weed for business and pleasure, burnt tires in the middle of the road, and little kids searching furtively for bush animals. An autochthon of the place was my tour guide for the time I would be spending there. For a little cash, she took me all around. I slept at a lodge meant for the Corpers, who were on break at that time. A small, but decent house. Two days I spent strolling, taking pictures. Then I saw a canal where kids sloshed through the discolored puddles looking for something. The water might be a mixture of sludge, animal waste and sharps. But these kids were oblivious of the danger, plunging their hands for the catch.

'Na their goldmine be that. You no *sabi* how much iron scrap cost?' said a man scanning the pile of dirt, also looking for something valuable. 'You fine well-well o.'

I noticed him staring at my cleavage.

The rain fell heavily. I stayed back at the lodge, checking out the pictures, sorting them. For days, the downpour increased. Boys in the area gathered more stones, adding to the riprap when they noticed the flood had trespassed the riverbanks. Coupled with news of crocodiles sneaking into the lodge at times, this convinced me I had to find somewhere safe. My guide told me of a school that required the service of an English Teacher. She suggested I could also snap pictures with them after lessons.

There, I met Yolanda. She came for morning class along with a few others. She became my favorite student and friend, too. Though older, Yolanda related with me like we were yealing.

I got to know that she had worked as a putter at *Ebute-Metta* railroad. Later she quit the job to do other construction jobs; filling, sanding, scraping asbestos from materials of older buildings. She worked as a janitor in between. Yoli was a man in a woman's body. She suggested I come live with her. 'I have a place. I can use your company. You don't have to pay rent. No *padi* for jungle. But I will keep you safe.'

I arrived at Tokyo-Villa. Faces scanned me. *Who be this one again o.*

It was Yolanda who first told me of the brownfield where the denizens worked before they were out of jobs. I asked Yolanda why she wouldn't leave this area for a better life in the city. She snickered, explaining she wouldn't stand a chance in an urban world. I knew it was a lie. She liked it here. The freedom to do whatever she wanted.

The flood increased. A surge damaged what was left of the rickety buildings void of people. The brownfield collapsed. The toxins mixed with the drinking water, making it unsafe for consumption. But Tokyo-Villa was safe, for now. Too many questions popped up in my head. Why isn't the government doing anything to decontaminate the brownfield? Why hasn't anyone heard about this? Who is going to come to their aid? I had many more questions to ask, but no answer. The bridge had been damaged. Canoe riders told of the risk in case you wanted to get past the boundary into the neighboring local government. I was stuck in Ajeshima.

Yolanda showed me how the hunt went down. Everyone called scavenging *hunt*. We walked past graffiti on the wall. I was ensorcelled by the equine drawing, white and red. We went to a machine shop. Choking motes suspended in the air greeted us, welcome. Mostly teenagers and a few aged worked there. 'Why are they not wearing masks?' I asked Yolanda. She laughed.

'They didn't die as children here in this locality. I am sure they can survive this.'

A man who I figured was the superior scolded a boy. His asperity made the boy shut off the drilling machine he held on to. The man poked the boy on the chest. Yolanda went over as though to settle the dispute, but I saw her cutting eye signal to me. Behind the superior's back, two boys carried three billets out the door. My best guess, someone outside received it, hid it for them.

Austin allows me to see Yolanda. I have roughly ten minutes with her before the management tells me to leave. Once a person is quarantined, only Austin and his team of auxiliary nurses are allowed to visit them until management says the patient's ailment is asymptomatic. I wear my N95, holding a wrapped package in my hand. Yolanda likes roasted grasscutter. She looks limp when I see her.

'Yoli, see what I brought for you.'

The aroma of the roasted meat wafts into the room. I unwrap it, cutting a chunk into her mouth. She chews on it the same way a baby growing teeth attempts his first bite. It breaks my heart to see her unable to eat. She asks if anyone has been threatening me in her absence. She asks of the garrulous Iya Ridwan who is pregnant with her seventh child. 'That woman jus' *dey* born like rat,' she says. We laugh about it. She asks about her goods, safely tucked inside her locker. Of all the things she asks, Yolanda never asks about her health.

'I have paid my bills on earth. When it is time, I will go,' she says, hitting her chest.

Yolanda got her fair share out of the billets stolen from the machine shop. I watched the boys who participated brokering a deal at a liquor store. She paid some of her share to a woman by the roadside selling roasted grasscutter and palm wine.

'Come. Let me show you somewhere,' Yolanda said.

She helped me climb up a pile of stones. The view was better from where we sat. The roasted meat tasted better than I expected.

Yolanda advised against drinking the palm-wine. A diurnal wind roamed, soothing my nerves. This area was completely different from the slum where the majority lived. The stench was minimal, though the breeze still carried scent of weed at intervals. I stretched my hands behind me, trying to relax, when my fingers touched a goop on a wad of newspaper. Yolanda couldn't stop laughing when she saw my hand. 'Na person *pikin* you touch so.' Someone had poured his semen there.

We got home to find a crowd before the façade of the building. A boy working in the machine shop had been carried away. He had a cold, which metamorphosed into something lethal. Yolanda knew him—one of the boys who helped in stealing the billets. We found out that some deposit of beryllium had taken his body hostage, damaging his heart in the process.

I went back to the machine shop the next day. Talking to the supervisor about providing masks for his workers, he asked if I would like a job as his personal assistant. The sick boy had been replaced. This one, too, exposed himself to the hazards without concern.

Home is where your heart lies. My mother has said this umpteen times. I wanted to be a lawyer, protect the frail people in society. Along the way I lost that interest. I entered for a degree in journalism, majoring in photo-journalism. This became my métier.

Yolanda kept going out for her regular hunt. One of these days, she promised, she would take me to where she worked. The hostel was boring. The few of us left in the room during the day were lazyish. A zaftig combing her wig sang in her local dialect. An old man tuned his radio set, searching for something of interest. I watched the ceiling, counting invisible stars. Ennui took over my sensations. My camera's battery was out flat. Dealers in batteries were at the other side of the river. There was no way I could reach them—the canoe driver was unavailable.

I asked around for anyone who deals in paper. *This is Tokyo-Villa. Everyone deals in every form of waste.* I went looking. On coming back from my short adventure, I found a huge of pile of newspapers, stacked it on my bed. 'Aunt be careful-o. Those paper been dey get bedbugs,' someone from the hostel said. I carried them outside. One after the other I began sorting them out, cutting out the images so I could paste them on the wall. It was high time this hostel got a facelift. Kids in the hostel joined me. Together we made art.

'Why do they call this place Tokyo-Villa?' I asked. One of the kids pointed to a gaunt old man chewing herbal stick, sitting on a straw chair.

'Sir, I was told you know the history of this place.' He coughed. Told me to grab a chair.

A group of people who regarded themselves as an NGO came to Ajeshima nine years ago. They had the goal of building a school for the inhabitants. Their leader met with the chairman of the association, relaying their purpose for coming. School was imperative, at least for the children. Other demands could be provided later. The project commenced. It was revealed that the Japanese who came with the group were the main sponsors of the project. The project went half-way, then resources were no longer available for completion. The old man said embezzlement took charge. Rodents, hoodlums, and miscreants saw the need to turn the place to a usual hangout. The association in Ajeshima came together, gathered resources, completed the building. This time the initial plan for the project changed: a hostel was built, named after the Japanese.

Yolanda came back at dusk. She was pissed at the paper arrangement at her bed space. She bloviated about how things were hard, the harsh situation. Here I was, wasting money on papers that I did not need. She thought I was obtuse. Someone has to keep hope alive. Perhaps mother earth would bring us good fortune in the days to come.

There are many rules in scavenging. The most important of them all is safety. We set out to *hunt* the following day. I replaced my camera battery after Yolanda bought a new one for me. We passed through a glen leading to a heap of disused items. Everything is useful in Ajeshima. Items abandoned in the open are left for vagrant dogs. We came across some boys and two girls in an effluent. Discharge from a severed drum plonked into the disturbed water. The teenagers were hunting for sharps. I rested my gaze on them. What if they get infected from this? Or worse, carry a vector to their homes. Yolanda shunned my rhetorical question. I noticed their change of mood upon discovering something riveting. It turned out to be a putrid animal, dead for days.

'Welcome to the jungle,' Yolanda said.

The next stop was a place that used to be an aquifer. It used to be the main source for good water before the pollution. Now the place had become anhydrous. 'What lies down there?' I asked Yolanda.

'Why don't you go down? I am sure the creatures living there will like human company,' she goaded. 'Put on your mask. We are approaching the area of Plant-17.' She said Plant-17 was responsible for the pollution. They dealt in a wide range of products from chemicals, fertilizers, metals, ceramics, and extraction of platinum metals to catalytic converters. The association had given them quick notice after having realized the damage they caused. Chaos erupted when the directors in Plant-17 employed the services of soldiers to stall the commotion of the people at their entrance. Property was damaged. At night the people threw bottles filled with fuel, gagged with a small piece of cloth, and lit on fire at the top. Two young boys were killed in sporadic shooting by the sentries guarding the place, and the hoodlums dispersed into the streets. An eye for an eye. The media got word of the happenings. Law enforcement came in mass, quelling the situation. Plant-17 took their leave abruptly. Police red duct tape couldn't restrict intruders from plundering what was left. They carted away scraps found in the building, leaving it in skeletal form. What they didn't know was that the company left a souvenir—cadmium residue in the air. The association banned anyone from going near Plant-17, noticing the number of sick children suffering from respiratory diseases. Yolanda a way around everything. 'This N95 will keep us safe,' she assured me.

'What are we looking for?' I asked, keeping my breath steady. A movement spooked me in the dust-covered, chapped papers to my left. A rat without a tail scurried across the floor with soot all over it. Yolanda said there were bad market days. I brought out my camera, taking shots of the rickety innards, piles of dirt. 'Yoli. There is something here.' She tightened her fur gloves, pulling up the trash to reveal fluttering cockroaches. One catalytic converter lay there helplessly. The smile on her face that day is etched deeper in my subconscious each time I remember. Yolanda hugged me, saying I brought her good luck. *Used catalytic converters are worth more than other scraps.*

On our way home, some men were goading a crocodile close to the effluent. This was not the first time I had heard of crocodiles coming into the open to find food.

Yolanda has reached her threshold of adverse health. I know this when the inhaler can't alleviate her anymore. The once-healthy figure I liked from the first day I met her has become shrunken. Austin says she has not been eating. Yolanda tells me of the severe pains sprouting from her body. Her fingers are clubbed, too.

I try to force myself to sleep that night, but I cannot. The room feels gelid. The mattress is missing a body. The atmosphere whistles a dirge. Austin's words thrum in my head. *She will need something stronger. Anything from flu or pneumonia treatments will make her better, temporarily.* 'Is there a cure for this sickness?' He shook his head. *There is no cure for it. She can live on an oxygen tank for the time being.* If what Yolanda needs is an oxygen tank, then I better give myself to that perverted representative of the elite group.

Yolanda summons me, to tell me about herself. She started fending for herself at the age of nine. Sold weed, drugs, did illicit jobs to survive. Her eyes show no remorse. *A girl must survive. No matter the cost.* She tells me where all her stash is. She is impervious to the thought of dying. 'Don't do anything stupid. It is time to start taking care of yourself,' Yolanda says. She points to my pimply face. Little speckles spread on my neck. I can't remember the last time I had a decent bath. It's been so long. She says I should promise her not to stay in Ajeshima if something happens to her. I could not hold back the tears from flooding my eyes.

Mother Earth answers my prayer. The rain stops pelting. The

flood still remains, filling the road, houses and shops. Austin calls for me. He needs to say no words.

I arrange the inhabitants of Tokyo-Villa, gather them for a photo shoot. One last look at Yolanda's bed. Memories we shared make me cry some more. As I walk across the repaired wooden bridge, I see children in the canal. The surface is turbid. One of the children is in pain. The others hold him still, pulling with their hands a leech halfway into an open sore in his foot. I snap a picture of them. Someone has to come to their aid. I can help with that.

The smell of good air is balmy, home. My sister snuggles me from behind. There is a lot I want to tell her. But first I hang the picture of Yolanda and me on my bookshelf, heading towards the bathroom.

Oyedotun Damilola is a Nigerian speculative fiction and pop culture writer. He likes to explore various themes ranging from the queer, war, ritual, environment, culture, and tradition.

His works have been published in *Okadabooks*, *Tush Magazine*, *100 Words Africa*, and in *Kalahari Review*.

Voice of God

Joseph Hope

When I was younger,
say twelve or thirteen.

I asked my preacher Dad
"How does God sound when he speaks to a mortal man like you?"

He said "Try to talk with water in your mouth,
multiply the rumble you make by infinity.

Try to read a message of inverted alphabets
arranged backwards and italized like birds standing on a rope.

Imagine the mighty sound of mega large trumpets or a line of
      horning cars,
a falling bridge, the squash sound as you step on a fat Roach.

As clear as mystery, his voice is the loudest
silence you can ever hear."

It's been ten years since then.
More bridges has collapsed.

And more cars are horning than ever
with the drivers more keen on moving in random.

Our troubles are multipled by infinity.

People have an inverted reasons for doing things that isn't right.
What a vile scene!

Last night rain made the reception bad,
my brother from the other end of the phone sounds like someone

whose head was under water
with mouth full of water.

The rumbling noise everywhere—
What is God saying?

Joseph Hope is writing from Nigeria, a student of Usman Danfodio University. His works are either forthcoming or already published in *Evening Street, PRAXIS Magazine, Spillwords, SprinNG, Writers Space Africa, Nthanda Magazine, Ariel Chart, Best "New" African Poets 2019 Anthology*, and many more. He's a young man running away from his name. How absurd! He tweets @ItzJoe9.

The Sun

SPF

Justine Teu

Apricot died, three days into the heat wave. She had just turned three, with no underlying health issues, but temperatures had soared to 120 degrees that weekend, and not even the full strength of Dani's air conditioner could keep the cat cool, much less alive. One minute, Apricot was a spry thing, young enough to live forever, and the next, she was gone, immobile under a bed sheet, claws still clinging to thread. Hugh, however, decided to blame no one, not Dani, not even the heat. It did not matter that thousands of pets died in the city that year, and it wouldn't matter how many more would die in the next. Even as Apricot's owner of three years, he would just fall back on his platitudes about the circle of life, hold back his tears, and talk about how her time had run out.

"What now?" Dani had said during the funeral in Hugh's Brooklyn backyard, while they were still digging up the plot. As a show of respect, Dani showed up in a black dress and a matching pair of sandals, while Hugh opted for an old-looking shirt with flowers splattered across the chest. In California, he insisted—though he'd only been a handful of times—people lived and thrived in their vintage finds, as if worn-down fabric could protect anyone from heat stroke.

"Who knows?" said Hugh. "Maybe she goes to the great beyond."

"The kind with white sand?" Dani asked, eying his god-awful shirt.

"*Kokomo,* baby."

"This is no time for The Beach Boys."

"There's always time for The Beach Boys," Hugh said.

"Not when a blizzard strikes in Zambia," Dani said, "and definitely not when the second one hits a month later."

Although Hugh never yelled, there came a crack in his smile as she brought up Zambia, an inscrutable knit in his eyebrows. He dug up the rest of the plot. When he buried the cat, he did not take his time in lowering her into the ground; he dropped her in with a quick *plop* that made Dani wince, then picked the shortest prayers to recite. Their moment of silence lasted a breath, a fraction of that, and then the service was over.

She walked home, he biked to the bodega. When she called later, Hugh insisted he was too busy to talk, and that he was getting ready to leave town for training camp again on the west coast. Dani knew better. The cat might have been at rest now, soon to be forgotten under the barren earth, but she would not die waiting for Hugh to admit the sky had been falling for a while now.

By next spring, Dani moved out from Brooklyn into her own apartment, west of Times Square. Rent in Hell's Kitchen was higher than she would've liked, the price of living alone on an island about to sink into the ocean, but she figured there was no better time than now; another heat wave was approaching this spring, with temperatures climbing to 125 degrees, and apartments were hot enough without another roommate or an extra cat taking up the space. Dani spent her nights mostly alone, content to bask in the air conditioning until the blackouts made them moot.

On one of those nights, Dani woke to the sound of her phone buzzing from the dresser.

"Dan!" It was Irene, the night before her shotgun wedding to a man who still bothered to take at least four kinds of daily multivitamins. She always missed the second syllable of Dani's name when she was excited about something. "Did the blackouts hit you?" she asked.

"Yes," Dani said. "About an hour ago."

"Oh you poor thing," Irene said with a click of her tongue. "Wasn't it only scheduled for the Upper West Side tonight?"

"They just keep getting worse," Dani said. "I have a theory, actually—that they're not planning them anymore. It's just everything going to shit."

"You're in a mood. You better not bring that to the reception."

"If I remember correctly, you just said I had to bring the napkins."

Irene laughed. "Well," she said, "why don't you sleep on my couch tonight? That way, you can just help me get ready in the morning."

"Sure," Dani said, "if you're sure Tom's still going to be there in the morning."

"That's not funny," Irene scolded. "I should just let you melt."

Dani laughed and the two of them made plans to meet up in about an hour. She got dressed, made sure her dress was still wrinkle-free in its garment bag, and slung it over her back. She packed away a few toiletries, deodorant, a toothbrush. Irene had makeup at her place. Hopefully tampons, too. In her pocket, she made sure to pack her 150 SPF sunblock, which she'd need when the sun rose.

Out on the street, a block party sprawled out up the street, to the edge of the intersection. They always followed the blackouts, in the neighborhoods where people didn't need or want enough to riot. Hell's Kitchen brought zeal; if they were going to be the next neighborhood to collapse into the river, they thought, let's just dance until doomsday. Residents brought out their battery-powered speakers and played thirty songs all at once, creating tunnels of bass so deep it felt as if this was the thing that might sink them. They danced from the fire escapes and rooftops in nothing but their underwear, while some even came naked with their pendulum genitals. They drank from their red plastic cups, spilling drinks onto the sidewalk in waterfalls. When things got really rowdy, people dropped various appliances from their rooftops, from toasters to TVs. People drove drunk in their chosen vehicles, racing their bicycles and mopeds at top speeds.

Tonight, the speedster was a tandem bicycle on the corner of fifty-second and tenth. Dani came within an inch of meeting her end when someone yanked her by the ankle and pulled her back towards the sidewalk. She let the cyclists curse her for trying to cross on a red light. In return, she delivered a middle finger in their direction, towards the horizon line, as if she were cursing it directly.

A laugh emerged in the air, close enough that it rose above the general noise. Maybe Dani knew the sound too well.

Hugh remained seated on the curbside, in a navy blue suit and a bloodied nose. Despite the starchiness of the fabric, the outpour, his smile grew with each passing millisecond, until it stretched past the crumpled napkin he held at his nostrils.

"Thought it was you," Hugh said, making a waving motion with his hand that lasted from the top of his head to the bottom of his chest.

Dani shrugged and pushed her hair back behind her shoulders. "I haven't had a chance to cut it."

Hugh stood up to meet her eye-to-eye, though he was a solid

six-two to her five-five. Dani resisted getting on her toes to match him.

"How have you been?" he asked.

"Fine," she said. "I'm on my way to Irene's."

"Oh, that," Hugh said with raised eyebrows. "I'm staying at their place, actually. Can you believe they're actually getting married? Don't you think they're rushing into things?"

"I don't think so," Dani said. Shotgun weddings were the norm in all her friend circles, even if the couples in question had been only been dating as little as a month. "It's—you know." She took one look at Hugh and remembered Apricot, the blizzards in Zambia, the new heat wave upon them. "Crazy little thing."

Hugh frowned at this for a moment, just like he had at Apricot's funeral, then nodded along as if to accept the answer. "Love," he said, as he removed the napkin from his nose.

"Anyway." Dani noticed the crusted blood at the edge of Hugh's nose. Pre-Apricot, she might have gone over to clean him up herself. Tonight, she would stay on the other side of the plot they dug up last spring, no matter how long it'd been since they filled it. "Isn't it a little early to put on a suit?" she asked, changing the subject. "The reception is tomorrow."

"I was on a date," Hugh said. "We were at a Broadway play a few blocks over. Then she said she wanted to walk along the canals."

"Horrible idea," Dani said. "People are always falling in."

"Some might find it romantic."

Just a year ago, the canals stretching across the odd streets were simply troughs filled with muddied water, an emergency measure to alleviate rising sea levels. *Romantic* was an attempt at outdoor seating, lampposts, and brick-lined sidewalks, enough to the point where people were calling the city New Amsterdam again.

"Did you know gondola drivers need medallions now?" Dani asked further. "Five million dollars a year."

Hugh made the sign of the cross. "God bless them."

"And where is she now? That poor woman?"

"She said it wasn't going to work out between us," Hugh stated with a sigh.

"Why's that?"

"She says I have nothing in my head."

"Well, that's wrong," Dani said. "You had blood ooze right

out of it."

Hugh laughed again. From the rooftops of Hell's Kitchen, illegal fireworks emerged like there was something to celebrate, and the two of them decided to make the cross-town trek together, along the canals.

In the morning, Irene put on her wedding dress and braided Dani's hair. She always insisted that Dani was the last girl in Manhattan to keep her tresses, and that it was a wedding gift in itself to be able to play with them one more time.

"I don't know how you do it," Irene said as she tied it up at the ends. Including the bride, every girl in the wedding party had some sort of short bob, or a pixie cut, while Dani had enough hair for it to hit the bottom of her breasts. "I mean, the length is easy to miss," Irene said, "but I always just have to tell myself that it's a chance to show off my collarbones."

"Like I said to Hugh last night," Dani said, "I haven't had a chance to go to the salon."

"Uh-huh," Irene said. "Weird that you ran into him, though."

"Yeah," said Dani, "like he just so happened to stay over the same night you invited me here, too."

"I had nothing to do with that." Irene yanked at a tuft of Dani's hair in retaliation. "In fact, he was the one to turn down this ritzy place his team was going to put him up in. He even told his manager, 'Stevie, I'm going to take the subway to Yankee Stadium. See you at batting practice later.'"

"What a waste!" Dani said.

"It's not everyday you get to have a wedding," Irene said, "and mine is going to be with a man I'll love until the day I die."

Dani looked out towards the living room, where she found the remnants of last night's sleep situation: two unmade couches, divided by a coffee table and a few errant coasters. Dani had taken one side while Hugh took the other, and the two of them had spent the night catching up, hushed under the rattle of the air conditioner.

"Tired of Brooklyn?" Hugh had asked, presumably about the Hell's Kitchen move.

"My roommate kept complaining about her ice cream melting. It was time to go."

"Oh?" Hugh said. "And how are you liking it now?"

"Well enough," Dani said.

"Enough to stay?"

"Sure. Where would I go anyway?"

"Jupiter?"

"Be serious."

"Out west," said Hugh. "Venice."

"Italy? That's east," *and sunken at the bottom of the Adriatic Sea.* Dani didn't say that last part.

"California," he clarified.

"I hardly have it in me to walk across the island," Dani said, "and you want me to move across the country."

"It's really not so bad."

"That's a shame," Dani said. "You've become one of those LA people."

"Oh, Dani," Hugh said.

"Yes, Hugh?"

"You should see me out there," he said. "I'm on TV every night."

Dani tore herself away from the couches, her time with Hugh. She found herself gritting her teeth. When Irene asked what she was thinking about, Dani merely called it the usual lack of sleep.

There were some people that electrified the rooms they walked into, and Dani knew countless girls that thought of Hugh in this way, and millions more would fall prey to him in Los Angeles. To Dani, it was more of an electrocution—teeth-gritting, lip-biting, shivering-in-a-heat wave sort of nervous system failure. He fried her, cut her, braised her for extra effect, even when he was merely asleep in the same room; memories lifted her into sleeplessness, soul out of body.

On the desk lay a few of Hugh's baseball cards, where he was featured as a backup infielder for the Los Angeles Dodgers. Irene tossed them over to Dani when she caught her looking at them from the bed.

"There's no point in fighting with someone who's in town for a few days," Dani told her. She couldn't help but scoff. "Baseball! The island is flooding, and all he cares about is batting practice."

Irene sighed, tucking a bit of hair behind Dani's ears. "You know how it goes. Some people are stupid enough to get married in this heat. Others run right in the sun."

The groom collapsed en route back to the apartment, just a few hours before the ceremony. The coroners called it heat-induced cardiac arrest, which made some sense: joggers everywhere were warned not to exercise out in the heat wave, but Tom kept on running just as he did every morning. It also didn't help that he'd been born with a defective heart, a fun fact he told Irene on their first date, but now all she could do was mumble about it in regret, as if she should've known she was marrying a man on borrowed time.

Hugh had been there. In fact, he'd encouraged Tom to go running that morning, even though he was hung-over from his bachelor party at the bar down the block. As Dani comforted Irene on the couch a few nights later, letting her wail into her lap, she stared at Hugh from the other side. It was Apricot all over again. The platitudes came like the eventual rain at the end of every heat wave, this one broken too early and for nothing: *he's in a better place, just know that he loved you until the end, things happen for a reason.* This only made Irene cry harder, so Dani asked to see Hugh in the hallway.

"How did he die?" Dani asked.

"Come on now, you heard Irene before," Hugh said with a swallow. "Cardiac arrest."

"You're missing a part of it."

"I mean, we don't know for sure it was caused by *that.*"

"Say it," Dani insisted.

"Who cares if it's hot?" Hugh said. "I mean, god, all those drills we run everyday on the field? No one breaks a sweat. Everyone's fine. We're always fine."

"It's not fine."

"He had a bad heart, okay?" Hugh's voice broke as he said this. "What more do you need to say about this? Just—he's gone to a better place. A better place than this."

"So you admit it, then," Dani said. "You know how bad it's gotten."

"That's not what I mean."

"Then explain it to me."

"It's why people leave New York," he said. "We don't have blackouts in California. We all still go to the beach and watch baseball after work. You know why I think Tom died?" He paused for a moment, making sure Irene was still inside the apartment. "It's because you're all counting down to it yourselves, like you're going to drop dead at zero."

Hugh took Dani's hand, which stunned her enough to hold his back tighter in competition. He kept his thumb pressed into the softest part of her palm, like he was trying to excavate her lifeline, or rip it apart with his fingernails. He let go and brought that same hand to Dani's cheek, where his fingers sifted through strands of her unwashed hair.

"You're not like them," said Hugh. "I remember Apricot. You put on your sunblock and you do all the things you have to. But you've still got it," he said. "And this city is going to rip it away from you if you don't do anything about it."

"What is it that I have?" Dani asked.

Inside the apartment, Irene stopped wailing, and all that remained were two people trying to breathe through the heat. Hugh held onto her, not by the hand, or a hug, but by the slight tug of her hair, looped between his fingers. Dani wondered, at that moment, if she should've cut her hair like the other girls. There'd be nothing to hold onto then, and Hugh would've had to settle for their natural distance.

The lights in the hallway flickered in and out until they went out altogether. Another blackout had arrived, and the people in their apartments began to holler and blast their music. Dani did not budge. In the darkness, she could still follow the lines of Hugh's body, upward to the arch of his nose and his sky-high cheekbones. She followed him until she was close enough to trace those lines herself. She pressed a thumb over his cheek, then the tip of his nose, his upper lip. She kept it there. Other people might have seen the blackout as some excuse to take off their clothes and consummate even the most fleeting of unions, but Dani knew not to push things. Irene and Tom had, when they first met and made love at a blackout down the street two years ago, and then when they decided to get married not two months after. Tom certainly pushed things, when he decided to go for a run in the middle of the city's worst heat wave ever. Dani knew better than to touch his face. This was not a consummation of anything. Repeating this to herself, she held the thumb over Hugh's lip like the lock to her old apartment, always jamming.

Hugh bowed his head, something Dani could feel when her thumb brushed back up the bridge of his nose. He embraced her, something he hadn't even done when Apricot died, or when Dani's father died. They remained that way as the tenants poured out of their apartments.

"Come to Los Angeles," Hugh said at last. "I'm tired of looking at you in the dark."

A downpour came after Hugh left, enough to render lighters useless and dampen any other plans for partying on the roof. Dani pawed her way back inside, where Irene busied herself by collecting all the balled up tissues she'd spent the day crying into. She didn't ask about Hugh, or where he'd gone in this storm, which was fine because Dani didn't feel like talking about anything at all. She merely followed after Irene in tidying up the apartment, lighting the tea candles that were supposed to sit next to name-cards and utensils, and cutting up her wedding veil into confetti. That was the nice thing about the dark, even the candle-lit kind. Dani could comfort with the best of them, all without letting Irene know that she had things to cry about, too.

Lastly, Irene mounted her portable speaker on the windowsill. She started "Come on Eileen", moved the couches to the opposite walls, and skipped around the coffee table. Her hands went up in the air as the chorus dropped. *"Come on, Irene,"* she sang with her hands over her heart, making Dani laugh. *"At this moment, you mean everything!"*

Dani could not help but dance, too. As she turned over and over around the coffee table, she let herself fall into dizziness, one that lasted hours and hours, and continued on until they were sure sunrise was coming.

In life, Dani's father had adored the New York Yankees. This was something he never had to prove to anyone, given the yearly pilgrimage he made to Florida, by car, where the team regularly held spring training. Dani thought this never made much sense, since the Yankees played in New York, plus the fact that the city hardly ever stayed cold enough to warrant a migration. Manhattan usually got one winter storm, the devastating kind with six or seven feet of snow and comet hail, before it all melted away as if it'd never happened by early February. Still, Dani's father never hesitated in packing a backpack, throwing on his favorite jersey, and leaving first thing in the morning. Then Dani would call him from the road, five minutes, maybe an hour later, and warn him of that year's approaching hurricane.

"Dani," he used to say, "there are just some things you shouldn't give in to." He insisted upon this even when the hurricanes needed new categories like seven, eight, sometimes nine. It was something Dani's mother used to say too, even in the throes of her skin-cancer-induced hospice care. Her Chinese family had a funny attitude about this: that no matter what, one had to keep good tidings, or everything else was going to catch up with you. This meant blessings from every elder before a flight, and the insistence that Dani should never frown on her birthday, even on the year her mother's hospice care turned into an empty bed in a hospital ward.

On her twenty-fifth birthday, the year after Tom's death, Dani found herself in a parking lot somewhere near the beach. She stretched her arms up to the sky after days of driving. Irene sat on the hood of her car, content to scarf down an extra large order of French fries. They'd been on the road for what felt like years, east coast to west, and all Dani could feel was a lingering queasiness, all the way up to her nostrils. She rushed behind the car and vomited right onto the pavement, where she remained crouched over her own mess.

"We reached the end," Irene said. "How could you still be car sick?"

Dani shrugged. She got progressively more and more nauseous the closer they got to California. "It's the fire," she said. "God, it was like driving through hell."

The entire state of California had been engulfed in what experts called the infinite drought. Everything from the air to the pavement to the rolling fields dried up, as if the entire region should've been cremated by wildfire. On the highway, inflamed skylines rose over the horizon, rising out of the trees and soaking into an orange sky. Out a rolled-down window, she had let her bare arm roam free in the open air, to sift the soot and ash. Her palm came back gray. In the constant light, she thought she look jaundiced.

Dani wiped off any remaining spittle and looked ahead, towards the wilted palm trees, the waves. The locals marched out towards the sand in their burnt skins, past the point of a supple pink. Fault lines formed across their faces, stretched and tight to the point of fissuring. Dani watched them—how they could still strip off their sun-safe clothes into bikinis and swim trunks. They bathed in the sea, not their sunscreens. The girls here still wore their hair long, longer than Dani's; they spread their arms open to the world, still with everything to give.

They drove further up the road, where they spotted a series of semi-attached apartments, all painted a shade of coral pink. The complex was called *The Ridley*. Dani had read on their website that it was named after the now-extinct Kemp's ridley sea turtle, and that one percent of the rent paid here would automatically go to some marine life charity the landlord designated. Dani doubted the credibility of this, but it was enough for Irene to justify the move across the country and claim she was doing all this for the greater good.

That night, when the two of them finished unpacking, Irene insisted on taking Dani out to dinner. Dani suspected this was out of pity. It wasn't like she'd had many people left to celebrate with in New York, since more and more of her friends had escaped to cooler cities like Boston or Toronto. Five months after Tom's death, Dani's own neighborhood had been re-zoned into sunken wasteland, thus ending her lease, which left Dani wondering why she was even playing this game of musical chairs with the other surviving Manhattanites. She imagined the lot of them, circling their ever-shrinking island, competing over apartments the size of linen closets. The whole endeavor, even the thought of it, was enough for both her and Irene to pack their bags and go.

"I'm glad we picked this place," Irene said, though she was the one who did all the deciding. She took in a deep breath as she locked their front door for the first time to drive to dinner. "It's going to be good things from now on. Making the most of it."

Dani inhaled, too; the air went down thick, balling up like a stone at the base of her throat.

"I wonder if it's why people wear vintage. It's bad, but in a good way. Like making the most of what you've got," Dani mused. "Like that one time Hugh wore this ugly Hawaiian shirt to a funeral."

"Hugh," Irene said, leaving her lips puckered. "Who needs him? All that boy does is hit baseballs."

Dani laughed, remembering their conversation the morning of the wedding never-to-be. She wrung an arm around Irene and kissed her on the cheek, thankful for her. For a moment, she pondered if all she would need here was Irene, and maybe that would be enough to sweeten the air.

At the restaurant in Santa Monica, Dani realized this was not going to be a dinner between the two of them. At the bar sat all the friends Dani once knew, most of them from college, meandering folk that only knew her through occasional social media updates and the rumors she once fancied Tom their sophomore year. No one could remember what she did for a living, or that Tom had died just before his wedding to Irene. No one recalled anything. They just sipped their drinks and nodded along, lost in the haze of forgetting something just as soon as they'd heard it.

Her birthday party stretched on for several nights; each reigned more sleepless than the last. One man who'd sympathized with Irene about Tom was now dancing close to her, to the point where it was inevitable they'd share a kiss. Dani braced herself for this, yet found herself nauseated when they made contact: she watched how their mouths fit so perfectly together, right at the start, then completely fell out of alignment. Irene yanked at his bottom lip like hardened taffy; he accidentally smattered himself across her cheek like he was trying to slurp a hot soup.

Dani ran out of the bar and threw up again, right on the curb.

She cursed wildly, out loud, twenty five times for twenty-five, and sat by herself on a bench. Her mind drifted to good tidings. As she peered up into the hills, fire lit up the peaks, a light of the worst kind. She let the sight of it mesmerize her, until she got three taps on the shoulder from behind.

It was Hugh. He smelled of spearmint gum, hair still wet from a shower, all of which Dani got to know up close when he hugged her briefly out of nowhere. She thought she was dreaming. On the car ride over, all the way from New York, she'd imagined bumping into him somewhere in the city. He'd be married to a model, or drinking a beer he'd be sponsoring on billboards. Instead of a cat, he'd have a bouncing golden retriever, appropriate for California. But this was no new moment. It was a moment that decided to pick itself up where it left off, as if Dani had pressed pause on it all the way in the East Village, carried it with her, and decided to let things play out on the other side of the country.

Dani shuffled her feet back and forth in silence. Hugh spit out his gum on the sidewalk and kept his eyes on the cement.

"Food poisoning?" Hugh asked.

Dani shook her head. "I'm not sure this city likes me that much." She pressed pause again, merely by stepping back from Hugh altogether. "What are you doing here?"

Hugh dug out a small box from his pocket and handed it over to Dani. Inside, there was a collectible pin, a "2" the size of a postage stamp. It was painted a simple white with navy blue pinstripes, the mark of the New York Yankees—and most importantly, the number of her father's favorite player when he was a kid. Dani resisted the urge to vomit again. Maybe it wasn't that. But she felt something in her was about to burst, so all she could do was shut the box and bow her head.

"I'm sorry," she said. "It's been weird, hasn't it?"

"Doesn't have to be," Hugh said. "We can pretend it's New Year's. Birthdays already feel like that, when you think about it. Whenever I break a resolution, I think, ah well, I'll just wish for things to get better when I blow out the candles."

"And does that ever work for you?" Dani asked.

"Maybe not all the other times," he said. "But you came to California, didn't you?"

That night, Dani abandoned her own party and drove away with Hugh with the top down, the city still burning above them. They ended up at the beach, where Dani encountered a west coast strain of those blackout partygoers. They were much the same with their red cups, their portable speakers; some things, like the need to dance, were universal. It was just the way they did it that felt foreign. In New York, the residents embraced dancing in the dark, feeling their way through the rest of the night, while the Los Angeles breed huddled around towering bonfires, as if the infernos had become part of who they were.

Hugh sat in the sand with her. Dani felt dizzy, just watching the people link hands and dance around whatever they could burn.

"I should be happy for her," Dani said. "I know I should." It was one of those things that rested, top of mind, like a book at the edge of a shelf. Normally, she pushed a thought like this back into place, to be forgotten like all the others, but she found herself unable to put it away. Maybe it was because Hugh wasn't dancing like all the others. Between them, there was a stillness she could speak into.

"But the whole time," she continued, "all I wanted to tell her was to slow down. Slow down, why don't you? You just met him. Tom just died." She peered out towards the shore, where she spotted the silhouette of a girl, dashing between the fire and the darkness of the waves. Dani thought someone should stop her, because she'd either get burned alive or swallowed up by the tide, never to be seen again, but no one did, and she kept running back and forth until the sight of her was a blur.

"I hate this place," she said. "But I can't hate you."

Dani let her eyes grow wide, impossibly so, and let out a childish yelp, something she used to do with Hugh when she couldn't make up her mind about certain things. He used to roll his eyes at this version of Dani, the silly Dani, but the sight of her this time made him smile, then wider, until it broke his face from the strain. She always knew when he was about to cry: the air currents around them changed, all by his attempt at a deep exhale, while he mashed his mouth closed so tight you couldn't see his lips anymore.

Dani, in turn, let their hands crawl towards each other until they were held. This was enough for Hugh break down altogether. He cried, ugly, then soft, until all he could do was smack himself to stop.

"Do you remember when we last met?" Hugh asked. "In Hell's Kitchen? My nose was all busted and that girl said I had nothing in my head?"

"Sure I do."

"Well, it didn't go like that. Not quite. She said she liked me, I think, but then I said I couldn't ever go out with her again. She asked me why."

"Why?" Dani mimicked.

"I didn't even know at first. It just fell out of my mouth. She was a perfectly fine girl, pretty, smart. Baseball fanatic. But I couldn't see her again. I just couldn't. So I told her, 'there's this girl who killed my cat last year, and I've never been able to forget her.' That's when she socked me in the nose and called me a pig. But I didn't care. I thought, *Dani has to come to California*—not because I was avoiding the end of the world. But because I wanted you at the very end of it."

"But then we walked the canals," Hugh continued on. "The way you belonged out there, like you knew every street still worth walking. The more I saw it, the more I thought, I have to save her. *I have to save her.* But then I knew there was no one to save. That that was the end of your world. And this here is mine."

Dani peered out towards the sea. The darkness seemed to stretch out forever, tides climbing higher and higher like they came out of the underworld itself. The girl, who'd been running between the light and the dark, had stopped altogether. The party stopped when they realized the girl was nowhere to be found, and that she was nowhere near the fire. She'd gone to the waves. Screams arose from the shore, with calls of a name Dani would soon forget, need to forget, for the sake of not counting another loss.

Justine Teu, a daughter to Chinese immigrants, is a Brooklyn-based writer pursuing her M.F.A. in fiction at The New School. She has forthcoming pieces in *Pigeon Pages*, *Menacing Hedge*, and *LEVEE Magazine*. Additionally, she is a first reader over at *khōréō*. In her spare time, she loves watching horror movies, caring for her eight houseplants, and wandering into liminal spaces. You can find her over at @justinecteu on Twitter, where she is probably tweeting about all these things.

Too Hot to Handle

Tracy Whiteside

[Images throughout]

Tracy Whiteside is a Chicago-area photographer specializing in Conceptual Art. A photographer for over 16 years, she is self-taught and is always developing new techniques. Her work has been seen in over 15 exhibitions and 80 publications in the last 2 years, including many magazine and book covers. With her current creations, Tracy wants to open your eyes with images of real people and the many aspects of their personalities that make them who they are. She uses Photoshop to achieve her visions. Inspiration is everywhere so she is always busy creating. You can enjoy her images on Instagram @whitesidetracyfashion and @whitesidetracy.

The Leaves

After Me, A Flood

Rae Kocatka

The engineer is kind enough, in that he lets Marin breathe his enriched oxygen. He lights something to smoke, lets most of it burn off into the room. The filters kick into high gear. *Filters.* Her lungs sear; her throat feels scorched. Marin holds her oxygen pack to her face with one hand and lets her father handle the pleasantries.

"You know, that's contraband," the engineer says, and Marin exists in a moment of pure terror. He winks. "I'll allow it."

Her heart knocks against her ribs and she gasps and tries to keep the malice from her smile. First impressions must be made.

The engineer holds out the deal with grimy, upturned hands. He calls them *industrial models*, and Marin's father laughs. They're remembering something, together, from earth. Two gears laughing at the clock they've been soldered into. They raise their voices in raucous laughter and for a moment, it's enough to drown out the hideous wheezing that's coming from Marin's chest.

The faux-lungs themselves are ugly things: dull metal, recycled ore, that early shimmery-soft bio-tissue that looks like liquid metal grafted together. She's seen patchwork fixes in the clinic, for miners with the goriest injuries—bones breaking through skin, crushed fingers, gruesome burns that go deep to the muscle. These are different; these are intricate. A faux-trachea shines with seams of blue: already cracked. They tremble in their case like living pieces of slag.

The medtechs have offered her months to live and carefully meted pity. This bargain is a bad deal. Marin is a bad deal. Too young to be in the mines, too damaged to ever earn out her contract topside. There is a scarcity to the air that is more marked for her than it is for the miners that file out of the tunnels at night, retching into their sleeves. Best case, she stops coughing up blood long enough to put in a few good years in the refinery before she's right back here, dying.

But her father has always been blind when it comes to Marin and his eyes are bright and the pen is already in his hand.

Don't you want to breathe? His favorite refrain. *Don't you want to get better?*

Marin doesn't want to be the one to tell him she's not worth his contract.

"Bet you'll be glad to get rid of those," the engineer says, pointing at her chest. As if parts of her can be plucked out and replaced for convenience's sake.

But these lungs are hers, and they're the only ones she's ever had, and she's not ready to be rid of them yet.

"I know they don't look like much, but I do good work. Stronger than those vanity models," says the engineer. "You can buy yourself a few good years." He flips the blinds and looks out at the bank of their little river, flush with cobalt dust.

He smiles, generous, irresistible, at Marin's father.

A few good years for who, she doesn't ask.

The violence of the surgery untethers her.

They're not a rich colony. The only surgeon is out of their reach, over on the light side. Here, they make do with expired supplies and good sense and self-preservative ignorance.

Marin sees herself on the table, anesthetized with contraband from the livestock facility, peeled open and glistening. The med-techs put her real lungs in a bin for disposal. They look like soft pumice, mottled and shrunken and pockmarked. The techs shuffle her, rearranging her ribs, her heart. They make room.

Put me back, she wants to say.

They take their time. They trace their fingers over the imperfect craftsmanship of her faux-lungs, mesmerized. They press on the bio-fiber just to see it clench and shudder, blow on the ends of the shining silvery veins to draw the color to the surface and watch it fade.

She is intensely aware of the moment the metal goes into her, matches up, slots together with her own self. A breathlessness, and then something almost as good as breath: a coolness, a relief.

There's something else, too: a blunting. A binding.

After, she claws her way back to consciousness alone in the

tent she shares with her father. Her center of gravity has shifted. She's heavier. Her new lungs feel huge in her chest, drag-anchoring her to the ground. Living tissue bears its own weight, at least. Her breathing is jagged, still, her chest distended and stiff. Her blood is a little darker, a little thicker.

The wrongness of it pervades her and she presses her hands to her chest and feels the solidity there and wonders how she would even go about ripping them out. She feels along her collarbone and hits bone in the wrong places. She settles into her newness. Acquaints herself with her transplanted chassis.

Despises it.

Her father is so pleased. He says she's the future. That she's lucky. He kisses her on the forehead and holds a stolen oxygen pack to her face, his own lips tinged with blue.

The week before Marin dies, the engineer's body turns up downstream where the water smells sour and the floodplains are buried under a foot of brackish grey sludge.

The colony doesn't break ground for burials. Shooting the dead into space is foolproof and cheap and Marin's been borrowing so much of her life for so long that she doesn't imagine it will happen to her any differently. The disposal techs talk about sending her remains back to earth for study, but there's another strike and the supply lines are all being rerouted. There's only room for one body amidst all that expensive dead cargo, and it's not hers.

Marin was nobody, so she gets zipped into a bag. She drifts along behind the techs, separate, bound, as they drag her body to processing. The metal detector trips when they wheel her through the bay doors. They pat their pockets, check the scanner. They look at each other and then at the body bag that has Marin in it.

The moment they cut into her and see gleaming metal lodged in her chest, she's salvage. Her own quarry. She doesn't blame them; they see some future they couldn't see before—inside her is the shape of baseless, desperate hope. Something to sell, something to study. Something to pass up the line to buy themselves a little more freedom.

She gets wheeled into another room, a lab where corpses go to be fed to the incinerator. They rifle through her bones and pluck the thing out of her ribs and sever the connections and then she is in two. She is scavenged. They carve her up, pull the cobalt trachea out of her, piece out the bronchi. They rinse it all until it gleams under the grey water sputtering from the tap.

She realizes, as they discard the meat-bits of her, that she has never seen a real, healthy lung, only imagined them: soft, pink, with feathery blood vessels, like the pictures in her moldy books.

I can't believe someone signed off on this, someone is saying. *Look at this vein, Jesus, who's refining this shit?* They pry their tools into her crevices. They tilt her body and scrape metal over her and eventually she's turned out into someone's palm. The warmth feels like the sun that's been described to her over a lifetime and she is handled with reverence, with tenderness.

Oh yeah, the technician says. *We can make use of this.*

Marin's never asked where the cobalt goes. Most of them don't. They're all consumed by the just-until-tomorrow's, the grind of it. Mouths covered until they can return to their little bubbles of stale air. Everyone falling over themselves to dig out that blue marrow for some stranger across the terminator line, across the galaxy.

Something of Marin is stuck in one of the new minerbots. Her new body creaks and shudders. Sometimes when the dust gets bad her joints lock up. Her plating is junk metal, the kind that hasn't been tempered right. Her limbs are too big. Her treads stick in the mud.

The only grace in this body is that it's inured from the poison that seeps out of the ground, that she is able to stand sentry while she watches everyone else sleepwalk toward messy, protracted deaths of scarcity. She records those: time, date, identification number, quadrant, corridor. She thinks it must be half programming, half self-imposed imperative: remember the ones who manage to escape this wretched dynamo. She looks for herself in them, but they're all caught up in their dying. The best she ever did was train for it.

She tries not to get lost in her seething jealousy, her awe for the way they all meet their ends.

She thinks she doesn't make a very good minerbot.

Sometimes, late at night, in her blue-lit alcove, she plays a game to try and learn this shell, to shock her new self awake. She focuses her will on trying to move its limbs forward. Corrupting its database. Writing directives of her own. Her speech processors aren't calibrated for screaming; the best they can do is translate her distress into a flat, garbled moan.

She sees a man that looks like her father, one day. They all look like her father: faces sallow and grey and crusted with poison, spitting the dust from their mouths. The man is trapped in a sinkhole. His corridor is flooding. He shouts at her. *Help me. You stupid fucking bot, do something.* But Marin's mouth is a slit and her voice is pre-recorded and all she can do is watch.

Stay calm, she chirps. Help is on the way.

She's decommissioned the next day when she coaxes her treads off the bridge and into the river.

She's being scrapped. She is torn and tossed into piles, she's threads and plates and cables and her memories blink and fade and she has to *choose* or she won't get to keep anything—

She is six. *We'll fix you right up,* her father tells her, the first time she becomes conspicuously ill. She's young yet, he tells her. She will get better. Right now, it's new. It's hard. The air is visibly thick; the atmosphere is thin enough that they dwell under a sky of eternal twilight. The storms turn dry and vicious as they blow in over the terminator zone. The dust kicks up cold, like the stories about winter back on earth. No snow, though. Everything that rains down here rains down grey.

He sees a future where she lives lives upon lives, the world she'll inhabit when she grows up. There's enough wonder in her still to believe him, to imagine that someday she might leave the dust behind. She has so much to look forward to, her father tells her. The mines, the planet, the adventure of it all. The colony will be different, so different, by the time she's grown—

Marin is in pieces, dumped in a bucket, onto a conveyer belt—

Marin is eight and her father crosses the line every day to throw out his back digging holes for the drill housing. He comes back slouching and stiff to kiss her on the forehead. He reads to her about history and time. He pulls pieces of stolen ore out of his pockets, lets her turn them over in her hands, holds them up to the light. This is better than air, he tells her—

—melted and pressed, melted and pressed, and still she can't find herself, *formless*, and she only has the shape of the memory of what it was like to have a body—

—she doesn't get better. Her father coughs, now, too. He forges her ID card on her birthday. He hands it to her and tells her she is a technician, now. The colony is hiring lots of technicians because the old minerbots from earth buckle under the gravity, here. They'll work it out soon. The colonists say this with awe, as if they are so lucky to be denied innovation. Like it's a great privilege to burn out your life in service of this dead rock, in service of other, better, luckier bodies somewhere else. The business is in the bodies, here. Use one up and the corps can buy another. Humans are doing the work of machines, always, paving their way. They are all just passing the time between now and when they cease—

Marin lies in the tent and listens to the oxygen recycle and imagines what it would be to fill a cart with cobalt and walk along the filthy tributary that feeds into the grey river without one hand pressing a mask to her face—

—she is rinsed, tumbled, rinsed. Formless is better, maybe. She warms. It feels like soothing and dark, like there may be an end to it—

—her father trades his rations for codeine for a week after the medtechs turn her away. His worker friends have to drag him back into the tent. She looks at the bottle in her hands, weighs the pain of bright hunger against the pain of seizing lungs. "Oh, dad," she tells him. "I wish you wouldn't." She isn't going to last the year—

—*fucked up the tempering,* someone is saying, *do it again*—

—she's eighteen and furious and holding a mask to her face between yelling at her stupid, naive father who won't *hear* her.

"You'll outlive all of them," he insists. He curls up on the floor on his mat, so scant beneath his filthy jumpsuit. He used to take up all the space in a room. He has withered into this stranger. "Just wait until they get the condensers working and we have real air," he says. "You'll see." You'll see.

He was right, almost. *Outlive* was generous.

Her body is laid in the stream bed and she's left to drown for 50 years.

She is some kind of pollution monitor nestled into the fine silt at the bottom of the river, a crab that's had its legs pulled off. She misses the sun. She is buried and flayed by tons and tons of rock and dust and filth suspended in the current. She's traded one life of drowning for another.

Sometimes there are human hands on her. This body is simpler than her last; it's not hard to trip the switch to shut the sensor off, to force herself to malfunction. Anything to attract their attention, anything to buy herself a few moments of maintenance out of the water. On these occasions she is drawn out and shaken before she is discarded again, her meter ignored.

The current rushes ever on and her housing fills with water and sediment. She goes unnoticed, tucked away from even the stars, her mouth soldered open in a silent scream.

They bury her in the walls.

Enough of her is here that she can thread herself through the wires. She must be in one of the administrative complexes. She finds the computer system unrecognizable, labyrinthine. The datacore gives her the current year and she laughs and rages, leaning on calcified muscle memory. She fries three of the door controls on level two.

It is nice to be touched, palm after palm laid against those control consoles. The soft press of a passcode is almost like a whisper;

the way they bend for retina scans feels like supplication. Even the momentary agony that comes with a short out is welcome. For the first time in years, she's *maintained*. They check her all the time. They go to great lengths to ensure her functionality. Her sensors are cleaned. Her interface demands constant attention and she is quietly thrilled with the new power she commands.

Her dominion is absolute. She can open the doors. She can deny entry. She can override the airlock controls and steal everyone's breath, flood their buildings with nothing, watch them beg and gasp and die.

She wonders at that. How she can still find fury, after so long.

She lets them live, she operates as expected. Clean people with clean clothes breathing clean air. She doesn't know how long she'll be here. She needs to be better than this monstrous system that has subsumed her. She needs to be able to tolerate herself. She hasn't looked in a mirror for a long time.

Her body lies fallow in a field.

It's the first time Marin has passed the terminator line. She didn't dare imagine it, in life; she's only ever experienced this side of the tidal-lock in the quiet space of stories and hushed whispers. The reality is grimier: she sits in a dried-up tidal basin, one of a thousand panels with their cracked faces turned skyward.

The sun soaks into her metal frame. She has few visitors. The dirt here is just dirt: inoffensive, inert. It stays on the ground instead of tearing over the plains in swirling clouds. She luxuriates in her frame of steel and weathered glass and cobalt, waits for the thin clouds to part so she can drown in the scant sunlight.

Her barometric readings tell her that the oxygen is abundant, now. Particulate matter has settled. The sky is the color of those pictures of junk cobalt, the pieces that weren't pure enough to be beaten into alloys. A stratosphere is forming. It is an embarrassment of riches. What lies they've all been told, over there in the dark. How constrained they all were.

To think they all thought they knew air.

She passes years without seeing a human. Overhead, the

transport ships skim the planetary rings streaked white over the sky, like someone has scraped away space itself. She dreams of the ascent. Of making it off-world. Of all of her, collected and brought back together and thrown gently into the same scrapheap.

They bring her back across the terminator line and her body is mounted on a launchpad and pointed at the sky.

It is almost a relief to be in the dark again. To be home. She is spread across so many pieces of metal, now. They have scavenged her from stolen scrap, and she is melted and cast and propped up on the hill overlooking the narrowest stretch of river. She is riveted back together and returned to herself and soldered into something strong and deliberate.

Hundreds of hands are on her at a time. Sometimes they come to her, alone, press their palms to her frame and whisper their hopes to her. It is almost warm, like skin on skin. So many of them must be dreaming for the first time. There is finally room to imagine what might be, it seems. There has not been a new engineer in some time. The ships have stopped coming. The river is a little clearer. These things they tell her. *Please work, baby,* they say. *This is it, I can feel it.*

She lets herself hope, for them.

She gathers, little by little, a sense of the future they intend for her. They tell her stories of escape. They tell her stories of the people they have held, the people they have breathed, the ones they've lost. She is to be a vessel; they will use her to leave this planet behind.

There will be no more dust and no more lungs and no more sky, but she is glad to be something more than slag to these hoping bodies.

She fails them. She never makes it past the fragile, fledgling cloud layer. She tries to stave off her reeling panic, but it spreads through her like the seizing of a diaphragm, the choking of phantom lungs. It shocks her metal into something brittle and shuddering; it shears away like sloughing skin. The loss of it all, the enormity of *almost,* drops her from the sky.

This feels familiar, too: she always gets so close. The sky recedes. The dizziness overtakes her.

The Corps burns the bodies before they dismantle her. They use her white-hot wreck as a pyre. She welcomes the scorching. She wishes it would take. But she's been breathing worse than smoke her whole life and she should know better by now: the lifeless parts of her always endure.

In her last life, she is laid into the circuitry of the dam.

Her body is wide and expansive. She holds back tons and tons of freezing poison, years, decades, centuries of the things the Corps has put away, out of sight, as if that lessens the violence of their transgressions. The reservoir runs through her teeth, cascades down the surface of her, thunders into the canyon below.

Her once-home is unrecognizable. She is distant from the parts of her that could tell her how long it's been. An eternity, certainly. She's built into the mountains she'd only ever glimpsed from the ground in that first life. The first time it rains, she thinks she's being demolished, the water stinging against her broad self. But then the barrage turns angry and bright and lovely. Almost too much after so long spent blunted and cold. She wonders if the atmosphere is suffused with metal, too. If there are places untouched by cobalt on this wretched colony. If it's still a colony or mostly a grave.

Open, closed, open, closed. She complies, this time. She plays thrall to whomever, whatever is controlling her. They must have learned better than to let her access their systems, or perhaps she is simply less every century. Perhaps every time she is diluted and melted and hammered into something new she loses something of herself.

One day, after a flood, bodies wash up against the base of her. Their blood rubs off on the piling; they stain her.

Her fury, muted for so long, reverberates through her, and she cracks. It doesn't take much; the poison has been eroding her for a long time. It drips down her face in a foul welter. There is more of it, and more of it. The waterline at her base disappears as the trickle becomes a torrent.

The river swells and spills over its grey-blue banks. It carries the silt, the shale, the bodies. It sweeps through the valley, forces what has been extracted back into the ground. All her life has been this: the dread, the waiting, the knowledge that she is failing, will fail. That her center is one breath away from collapsing. That the most she can do is hasten her own collapse.

She can drive mercy towards them. Out of herself. She wants them to know, just once, what it feels like.

The trick has always been the same: keep breathing.

Marin groans and heaves. Sighs. Lets the deluge cleave her.

Rae Kocatka is from the woods. She is a writer, seamstress and cosplayer, and full-time dog guardian. Graduate of the 2018 Clarion West workshop. Currently moonlights as a swamp thing. Follow her @raetroll on twitter, or at raekocatka.com.

letters from the ides

Jennifer Mace

I am writing to tell you
that the apple blossoms have opened
and, for a moment, made clouds
out of the trees. rain has swept
the cherry's petals
into great muddy drifts
where they will linger, for now,
in a deficit of brooms—or rather
of hands and arms to sweep them.

we are become molluscs, in a way,
curled up soft and moist
within our shells. sound
reverberates a little differently
through homes turned castles;
I press my cheek against the wall
when the twins cry, learn to recognize
their parents' footsteps.
a world away. connected.

I try to think of us as coral.
the city, that is—a thing
of shell and rebar, concrete,
glass and grass and promises.
even as polyps retreat
against the coming storm,
we breathe and breathe and
breathe. creatures, for once,
made flesh; and in that, unified.

but you have to understand:

I try to think of us as coral
because the alternative
is to wake in the night
as red blood cells, as marrow,
as the dna-test scrapings
off the inside of a crime scene
while the skeleton of Seattle
struggles on without us—because
if there is anything to learn
from the rot and rent of centuries,
it is that even bones can crumble,
given time.

fear is a nebulous companion.
I did not invite it in. and yet
we are none of us hermetic, none
immutable under strain. I fear
this is a chrysalis. I fear
what might emerge. I fear
more than anything
that it will not
be enough.
I fear

that the deaths
and the wounded
will dissipate
from our memory
as atrocity so
often does, and
leave us frozen
by a future we
cannot prevent.

I fear it will
happen again.

but I
am not
my fear.

I *will not be* my fear.

and so:

I am writing to tell you that
today, I saw a robin. it clung
to the corner of the sidewalk
and pecked at leaf mulch
caught in the unswept gutter.
worms, I would imagine, had emerged
after the rain, and the bird,
appropriately, would eat its fill.

today, the sky was blue and chill
over the white and pink of flowers,
and the streets, new-washed, stood empty
as at dawn.

in the quarrelling gulls and crow mobs
where our footsteps used to tread,
I must see courage: I must take of this
a caring, a patience, a love
for one another, in this organism city,
that faces the gaping unknown future
& says: together. we will wait, and watch,
and see what comes, and tomorrow, perhaps,
the maple may bud, and perhaps
we will see it
with you.

Jennifer Mace is a queer Brit who roams the Pacific Northwest in search of tea and interesting plant life. A two-time Hugo-finalist podcaster for her work with *Be The Serpent*, she writes about strange magic and the cracks that form in society. Her short fiction has appeared in *Cast of Wonders* and the anthology *Skies of Wonder, Skies of Danger*, while her poetry may be found in *Liminality* and *Uncanny*. Her anthology *Silk & Steel: A Queer Speculative Adventure Anthology*, with co-editors Janine Southard and Django Wexler, may be found through Cantina Press. Find her online at www.englishmace.com.

Photo credit: Karen Osborne.

The Restoration

Karen Heuler

They'd been restarting the earth for over five years now.

Marie picked up a box of seeds and some jars of bugs and soil bacteria from the dispensary. They gave her hackberry seedlings too, a good, hardy tree. She put all these things in the large panniers on her bike. She was instructed to go north and west, and she went by train to her first stop, where she switched to the bicycle and set off until she found a house beside a dry riverbed. It was probably once a vacation setting. She leaned her bike against the house and went up to the front door and knocked. No one. She went on to the next house and the next, until she found someone at home at last.

"I'm from the Seeding Project," she said. "Can you take the seedlings for three trees? I've got some worms, too."

An old woman stood in the doorway. "Trees," she said. "Yes."

They went around to the back yard, which was dry and had a small section fenced off for a vegetable garden.

"What are you growing?" Marie asked, indicating the plot.

"Beans, sometimes. I get a few tomatoes, too. Not much, it takes a lot of water."

"Can you handle the trees? They're hackberry. They can tolerate drought when they're full grown, but they'll need water for the first year or so."

"If they're close to the house, yes. I get some water from the well, mostly in the morning. It trickles up again overnight. I store some for the plants and I water them in the evening, so it won't evaporate right away. There were trees when I was younger. It was wonderful to watch them in the storms, you know. And hear them. Yes, I'll take the trees."

They chose spots for the trees, dug holes, and planted one seedling for each hole. She helped the woman measure out a gallon of water.

"Trees," the woman said, and her eyes were bright.

"Someone will be along with groundcover in a few months," Marie said. "And some beetles after that. Try to keep everything fairly close together—I mean, to form a habitat. But you know that."

"I do," she said.

She was invited inside for water and something to eat. A protein stew. And then Marie moved on to find another house.

On the first day, she planted nine trees, and logged the addresses in. The next day was only six trees, because the houses were farther apart. One day she couldn't find anyone who would agree. One man was moving on; some houses were shut up. She found a heritage farm with two old horses and a dog. The man there pointed to the unworked fields. "What about them?" he asked. "Do you have any corn?"

"Not enough rain for corn," she said. "I've been doing this for five years, and they've never had corn." She saw the look on his face. "I'll make a note. Maybe the rains will come."

The owner of the next house was very friendly. "Ah," she said, "A bee man came by a few months ago. I don't like bees much, but I took some. They're living near the house. Not too near," she said. "And I don't have to water them or anything."

"Good. And are you composting?"

"I even have worms," she replied. "They came out of nowhere. I put scraps in there. They like it. I'm supposed to turn half of them into the soil in a few weeks, then build them up again."

"I can give you two more worms and maybe some squash seeds."

She logged all this, and sat down to a welcome meal of water and a sandwich. The bread was dense and therefore government issue. The paste was probably beans and whatever fish was raised on the fish farms. Probably some parsley mixed in, easy to grow. It made her drink more water, however, and she apologized for her thirst.

Marie was tired and sat for a while, looking at the sky. The woman was friendly and sat with her. There were really only two ongoing conversations these days: "When I was a child" and "They say in fifty years." The woman chose the latter.

"They say in fifty years we might have trees and maybe more crops. I won't be here, of course. They sprayed a lot when I was a kid, but I remember what it was like."

They both paused, thinking about it. "I may not be here when the trees grow tall. But someone will see them." She said it with satisfaction.

They sat companionably together, until it was time for her to leave. Marie stood to go and the woman raised her head up, her face lined with worry and said, "And the predators? Have you heard when they'll release the predators?"

After five years of releasing things one by one, trying to restore the environment from the bottom up, everyone kept asking about that.

"What have you got there?" a man asked suspiciously, farther along.

"It's just some cocoons."

He eyed her warily. "Poisonous?"

"Are any cocoons poisonous?" She was startled.

"Not the cocoons. What comes out."

"No. It's just some moths and a few fritillaria. Perfectly harmless."

There was another cautious silence. "So," the man said, dropping his voice even lower. How low could it possibly go? "When are they releasing the predators?"

She had learned how to unnerve people by looking at them with absolutely no expression. She'd done that just to do it, for no good purpose. She liked to test things. If there had been snakes in her childhood, she would have prodded them with a stick. She would have whacked a hornet's next. She would have leapt off cliffs. The closest she could come to danger and adventure was this, sticking cocoons to the undersides of houses, or on bushes someone a year ahead of her had planted.

"The predators," she said. "They did mention them. Soon, I think."

"Big cats?" the man whispered.

"Bred to be big."

"Bears?"

She shook her head. "Too hot, they said."

"Alligators?"

"I think I heard that. And, I think—hippos? I hear they have a temper. Of course they like the water, which means that you take a chance if you find a river. But that's the point, isn't it? To even things out?"

"There's no river here," the man said, relieved. "I have a well. And there's a mud pond when the rains come."

"Oh well, I'm sure a mud pond would do," she said evenly.

The first wave of Seeding had been worms and some bacteria and micro-organisms for the soil, and then small bugs and grasses, and clovers and seeds of all kinds and then more bugs and then lizards and birds and small mammals, going up and up. Wild raspberry, different bushes, chinkapin oaks, one wave after another. Squirrels, chipmunks, raccoons, rabbits. Up and up. Soon there would be deer and coyotes and some wild ponies on the best plains sites. Eventually, cougars, rattlers, venomous insects, poisonous plants. A fair playing field, was how it was being described. The world had gotten destroyed by the apex animal, and it was because the apex animal had been unchecked. So bring back the checks. Make it fair. No one was very specific about the final predators, the ones who would help to keep the people in check. Lions; wolves; what?

The complaints against the top predators had been loud, but the decision had come at a time when the world's resources were at the lowest point. People were dying of hunger, of thirst, of disease in a world that had been squeezed too tightly. They would face the predators when they needed to, but even before that, they needed to eat.

Marie found a platform rising from a flat plain. She dropped her bike and walked around it. There were fourteen wooden steps up to the top, no railing on any of it. It wasn't very old, so it likely wasn't a hunter's blind left over from the good times. There were no hunters now, anyway. Guns had been confiscated, poisons and traps as well. Unregenerate hunters had been rounded up and housed somewhere far away. The whole point now was to let everything try to live.

She climbed up and looked around. Mostly dry floodplain, but off to the right were one or two tall trees, and some scrub bushes and tall grasses. The beginning of something, she thought. She'd add some bees and spores before she left. Flies, too.

Far, far off she could see the grasses moving, left to right. From this distance, it was hard to imagine how tall the grasses were, and how big the creature might be. A raccoon? A possum? It made her uneasy, this creature she couldn't see.

She went to a small farm where she was let in and gave them the seeds and worms and was asked to stay for dinner and then, as the sun set, they offered to put her up for the night, as long as she left first thing in the morning and didn't shower. "We're using more water because of you," the woman said gently. "And we need it for the vegetables and of course for the seeds. And the chickens, too." Dinner was eggs and some potatoes and some herbs and a mushy protein.

"How are the chickens doing?'

"Better, since they brought those beetles last year. Though the birds disappear sometimes. We don't know where they go."

"Do any of them ever come back? You know, just find something interesting while they're away and then remember home?"

"No. They're gone. They're good and gone. We think, sometimes," and here she hesitated and looked over to her husband. "We think sometimes that it's the seeders. We know they have to eat and we know some of them are, well...shy. Not given much to social situations."

"No one's allowed to *kill*," Marie said patiently. "That means us, too. Killing harms the earth. Maybe later, when there's an abundance—if there's an abundance—maybe then killing animals will be permitted. But slaughter belongs to the past. I can't imagine anyone doing it."

"I can't imagine any other explanation. I mean, they have to eat—you have to eat."

"No," Marie said, intent on getting this woman to stop saying this—stop thinking this. "Really, the seeders are fine. They're tested, you know. To make sure they fit the job."

The husband snorted. "We had problems with the centipede guy," her husband said grumpily. "He wanted to come in for a glass of water and we said of course, and well—he unloaded a bunch of centipedes in the house." He glared at her. "Did he have to do that?"

She had to keep herself from rolling her eyes. "Centipedes walk around. Maybe there's a hole in the foundation or near a window or somewhere. At any rate, I'm sorry that happened. But it has to go on, you know. We can't be the only living organisms on this globe."

"I know," the man said abruptly. "No need to lecture. Just—whatever you have, keep it outside." He got up and left the table.

Occasionally, she happened onto a thriving community with wells with good water, with plots of land that grew food and even some cows and chickens and goats that hadn't been provided by the agency. It was a microgeographical heaven. There was birdsong and there were bugs flying—and fleas and mites and mosquitoes and other things that she had tended to forget about. This is what life was like, both good and bad, beautiful and irritating, all flowing together. No bug sprays. No weed killers, no polluted water. Cow dung for fertilizer. Solar for heat and cooling. This was the way it was supposed to work.

"It's so wonderful here," she told the family she was staying with. Farmers and teachers, the two most important professions.

"Don't tell anyone!" the woman yelped. "We're supporting ourselves at this size but I think we'd get into trouble if there's any more people."

"Of course not," Marie said, soothing her. "Of course not. We're not allowed to discuss locations, anyway. You're safe. I'll just be here for a few hours and I'll be on my way." It was, after all, a kind of rehearsal for restoration. A wonderful, brief dip into the future.

"What are you putting out?" the woman asked.

"Ticks."

"Ticks? What, are you crazy? We don't want ticks." She stood up and put her arms akimbo. Defiant.

"Oh but ticks have a place," Marie said. "Birds eat them, you know. Chickens especially. And possum."

"We don't want those either!"

"Why not? They eat ticks."

The woman's mouth dropped open and then she laughed out loud. "Oh now I see, I can tell you're messing with me."

"I am," Marie said, grinning. "But you've got to understand that I have all this time in my head when I'm going from one place to the next. So I think up things to say to people."

"You shouldn't," she was told. "I mean, people get a little off when they're alone too much."

Marie shook her head. "People get a little off when the worlds ends. You know?"

The woman sighed heavily. "I know. But no ticks."

She had been out for two weeks, with some days almost silent, marking deserted houses. In those cases, she walked around them, noting anything growing, pulling leaves if she couldn't recognize a plant, listening for bird song and frog croaks and any signs of life. She found a house almost filled with spiders. It was not something she was likely to forget. She found spiders repugnant. She dreaded them. She had had to reassure herself that there was little chance that any spider she encountered was dangerous.

She thought that the first lacey sheets were spider webs but in fact it was the daddy log-legs, their legs linked, forming a chain of curtains that rippled without wind. She had yelped. She had run outside and dusted herself off and when that didn't help, she removed her sweater and shook it out and then took off her shoes and socks and shirt and shorts and shaken everything out until she was satisfied that nothing remained on her.

It had taken a while to regain her confidence but she had continued with her mission, though she didn't go back inside. She walked around the house and found two wolf spiders, lurking as they usually did. Unpleasant creatures. She had buttoned her blouse up to her neck and continued cautiously. Wolf spiders liked to be near water, so she looked for a pond or a leaky pipe. She could hear water trickling, and traced it to a corner of the house, where either an underground pipe or a small stream pumped up bubbles of water. She planted three trees there herself, looking over her shoulder and around constantly. No one would have to be responsible for watering them. At least finding the spiders had led to something good.

Had the spider man been here or was this some sort of natural selection? She was aware that, in nature as it used to be, sometimes things would explode into excess and sometimes disappear into extinction. This particular extinction had been casually made by human greed. She made a note to ask if someone had deliberately left those spiders. She didn't actually know which answer would bring more relief.

It was late spring, and heat was coming on so she changed her biking to morning and evening, which is what people did as the temperature rose. She stayed with a horse rescuer, a metal worker, a mechanic, a blacksmith, a baker, some kids who had run away and had found an empty house. Different people. Some of them wanted seeds; some did not. She was not judgmental; the seeds were a commitment and not everyone stayed put.

Once she saw a hawk overhead. She stood there mesmerized. What was the hawk hunting? She thought it might be mice or maybe even rabbits; the rabbits would be quick to multiply. That cheered her up, that things were thriving. At her next house she asked about that, about hawks and rabbit and got a slow nod. "Someone brought rabbits and let them go. Not your people, just some, I guess you'd call them free-lance? There's that going on. People who saved seeds you know about, but people also had pets. Or places where things held on."

"That's great," she said. "I watched the hawk for a long time; it never dove. But it was looking and I have to think it had a reason for that."

"Most likely," the man said. "Most likely."

It didn't occur to her until a few days later that a hawk was a predator. Of course it was, she knew that. But she had been thinking that the release of predators meant things that would threaten her, and a hawk did not. And besides, weren't they supposed to be warned? She thought about that as she wheeled her way down a driveway, left some seeds and then went on. The people there had been nice. They said they'd seen a snake, but they believed it was a ring-necked snake, a small one, maybe a baby—not a litter, what was the word— and what about cats? When would there be cats again?

She would love a cat. After her tour was over, she hoped she would meet a nice man and they would live together and have a cat. Maybe they'd have a kid, too, though she'd have to see what the world was like in a few years.

She was due to check in to a Service cabin, only a few miles away. They were kept stocked, so there'd be food and water and beds and, of course, new seeds to take with her and a counselor to advise her on her next steps. She'd stayed with people the last few nights, but it was hard to use their water and eat their food. Everyone struggled. But the cabin would be well-stocked because it was intermittently used.

She made a quick decision to try to get there before nightfall.

But she timed it wrong; within an hour it was getting dark. She was off the main road, cutting across a dry-grass field to get to the cabin, and she could no longer bike. Pushing the bike was hard work, and slowed her down even more. It had been a long, slow afternoon but then all at once it was racing towards sunset. She consulted her map and her GPS and figured it was another hour or so. She looked up. A few clouds. If the moon came out, that would help. She checked the moon chart. Sickle. Not much light.

It was her own fault, and besides it was warm. If she didn't make it, she would sleep outside; she'd done it a lot already.

The grasses got taller and thicker and she couldn't see the end to them yet. She stopped, took out her canteen, took a sip of water and put it away. She took out the knife she carried and used it for a while as a machete—or tried to; it wasn't very good.

It was tiring. She stopped and thought about staying right where she was. She could easily push a wad of the grasses down and cover them with her space blanket. She had some protein bars and enough water to make them go down easily enough. She kept checking her direction and lighting the way ahead of her, but it was wasting the phone's battery. Best to stamp down the grasses and spend the night where she was. In the morning she could get to the cabin and have breakfast and a wash.

She made a decent bed and spread out her blanket and was eating her health bar when she saw a light in the distance. She paused in the middle of a chew, thinking. Was this the cabin or was it someone's home? It was risky to knock on a stranger's door at night, even though the guns had been confiscated. People were erratic. Just then a shadow passed in front of the light. It seemed bulky and it paused at the window. She imagined him staring out at her. Looking for her.

She listened for the whistle of grasses moving, for the lurch of an animal footstep. What was she expecting? The world was safe. There was nothing alive anymore that could kill her. Except people of course, other people. Was that what she was worrying about? That man whose shadow she'd seen—was he somewhere close by, sniffing the air for her, creeping up on her? She'd been out in the field for a few years and yet she'd never truly felt afraid. Angry at the way the world was; regret for what had been done; hope a few times, hope for what she could accomplish; but never really and truly afraid.

What was she afraid of? She was alone in a field of grasses, with bugs at her face, bugs that she should be grateful about. She looked ahead and saw the light had gone out.

Something flew by her in the night; wings. Were there owls? They had released mice and there were apparently rabbits. And that hawk the other day. There was beginning to be an ecosystem, no matter how limited.

A bug crawled over the hand that held the knife. And then another one. Were they really there or was this just nerves? Now there was something on her neck.

Something was moving in the weeds, moving closer. She listened intently, willing herself not to brush anything off, afraid that any sound she made would draw whatever was out there. Was it an animal or was it the man from the house? Surely it would be a man, not a woman. No woman did that—stalked someone in the dark. Why didn't women do that? There was something on her face now, crawling around her nose. Now it was moving towards her eyes. She closed her eyes tight.

Something bit her and she drew in her breath despite herself. The rustling paused. She felt a creature waiting out there for her, listening for her. She could feel eyes peering at her in the dark, sniffing for her, even.

She lay there, curled up, all night long. She dozed off for brief minutes, jerking herself awake, and even then not moving at all for fear of making an identifiable sound.

She woke and stood up slowly and looked around. The grasses stretched away. There were the beginnings of small trees, then some bushes and off some distance past them, a cabin. She squinted. She had been much closer than she thought.

Her nerves were on edge and the hairs on her neck prickled. She carried her seeds and some bugs and she moved slowly and carefully, observing everything. There was birdsong; and it stilled when she got near. If it weren't for the fact that she had been thrown off balance, she would be reveling in this. It was what they were all working for: a bit of the earth that had life in it. She made her way across the field in the daylight, walking slowly and pushing grasses aside. There were more and more insects—she stopped and checked them and saw grasshoppers and beetles. An amazing crop, really. They'd been seeding bugs for years now but up to now she'd only seen a few, and not much variety. This valley showed what could be done and how quickly it could be done. She wondered how many of the people from that village she'd passed came here. She hoped they hadn't actually found it—or if they had, that they would respect it and allow it to develop.

A man came out of the cabin, saw her, and gave an exaggerated wave. He cupped his hands around his mouth and shouted something, but she couldn't hear it until she got closer. He kept saying "Watch your step!" but he didn't say why, so she stopped and looked around, expecting rocks or fallen outhouses with nails sticking up. She saw nothing, but she slowed her step and walked forward, casting her eyes about until she came out of the fields into the clearing around the house.

"Snakes," he said in explanation.

"Ring-necks?" she asked. "Garden snakes?"

He laughed. "That's a good attitude," he answered, which puzzled her even more.

"I was expecting you last night," he said. "Run into trouble?" He led her into the cabin, which had three other Seeders in it, Malcolm, Zach, and Jenny. Seeders loved to meet each other, so they asked where she'd been, what she'd seen, what she'd heard, and she asked back.

Alex was the outpost leader, a bald black man around 50. He waited patiently for all of them to finish and settle down.

"Well, you're a day late, but that's all right," he told her. "You're actually down for a two-day break—all of you are—so there's time to catch your breath before you head on out again. Actually, I'll be heading out with you. This particular area is considered far enough advanced that we can let it go for a year and then come back and see results. We'll switch to the barer areas." He grinned. "You say that: barer areas. It's hard." They laughed genially.

He sort of looked away and then looked back. "I'm curious what you've all been hearing from people, so let's take a little time to go over what they've said, and also let's discuss what communities there are and where they are and what their water situation is, for instance. Just a general sense of what's out there now. You'll be filing with the office if you haven't already, but I'd like to get us all to look at the bigger picture right now."

He nodded and motioned to them one by one. She was interested in their stories. There were areas with nothing out there— abandoned houses, dried-up wells, that sort of thing. But there was also a loose wide circle of places where people were resettling and bringing in a cow here, a goat there, even two horses. People, generally, who had lived there before and kept an eye out. Who had hoarded the few animals they had left and the seeds they had gathered. The animals were of course precious because they produced good fertilizer, if there was enough to feed them. They had resettled a year or two earlier, from all accounts, and some people now had babies. They were small communities, but they radiated hope. The seeders talked about what life had been like before it began to slip away; this was what they'd been working towards. They nodded to each other, their eyes shining. They just handed it around, their visions of a renewed world, a green world.

Alex encouraged them. "Beautiful, isn't it? Like life used to be? Yes? I remember it, myself, I grew up in the country and then we moved to the suburbs. Never having to think about anything, really. Food and safety and water, heat when you needed it, a/c when you needed it. Go to a store and get what you want. Get in a car and go where you want. Good days, right?"

They got still, the good memories slipping from them. They knew where he was going.

"Of course, everything pretty much died to give us that. The wilderness, the prairies, the forests, the wild animals. Extending our own secure zones by destroying theirs. Doesn't seem right? It wasn't right. So we can't reproduce that. We have to be careful that we get the balance right."

"It's time?" Zach asked softly.

"It's time," Alex said. He looked behind them, at the distribution boxes. They all turned and looked at them, shifting slightly, their shoulders tightening.

She hadn't thought it would be this soon. Well, none of them had. This part had been in the future—she thought long ahead in the future, nothing to worry about now.

But there had been signs, of course. Those movements in the grasses—there was animal life. Those thriving homes, with children. That sudden fear last night was not a vestigial fear; it was the animal in her acknowledging that there was a threat roaming, moving, reaching out to her.

"What is it?" she asked. "What are we releasing?"

"The middle. Not the big things yet. Venomous snakes and

spiders. African bees. Mosquitoes and ticks with diseases. We've already got a few souls out releasing the smaller cats—puma; civet. It's just the beginning, really. I don't think any of us will die from it." He looked at them. "You knew it was coming."

They nodded and murmured agreeably. They were trying to look at it as a good thing. But there was a part of them that fought it.

"We can't make the same mistakes," Jenny whispered. "We have to make sure that there are constraints on us. We have to make sure we're actually part of the cycle of nature. We moved out of that a while ago."

"We know," Malcolm said stiffly.

Zach looked a little happy about it; he had a small smile. "I like snakes," he said. "I'll take them."

She looked around at them. Eager or not, they had a look in their eyes that they were committed to this, and she supposed she had the same look. It was calculating. It said, "At least I'll know, and I can be careful. At least I'll know."

She had to orient her emotions, for a moment. She knew the others felt the way she had up until now—that the predators were the future, not the present. That they could be brave in their resolve for the future, but that bravery wouldn't be tested. Because the world, half destroyed as it was, was also fairly safe for humans as far as immediate threats were concerned. There was nothing to harm her. Yes—drought was a persistent problem, and the results of drought and the lack of animals and insects and birds were the results of a decline in the productivity of the earth, but she personally had access to food and water. She could think about danger and threat in an abstract way. This, however, was immediate and personal and not abstract.

Zach was still cheerful, but the other two were quiet and were probably lost, as she was, in thinking about the days ahead. Up until now they had been restoring what was essentially benevolent, the little things that parsed the earth. Now they were being turned into the first wave of checks. They were the beginning of a leveling.

"Well, that's it," Alex said. "We'll have a relaxing evening and in the morning you'll be off. You'll get the usual map with directions, and if you want to choose a box rather than have it assigned to you, go right ahead. I know you have mixed emotions—you're not the first group going out with these. I can tell you that this step is truly and remarkably necessary. We'll be going out with the big cats and the bears and stuff pretty soon, and there will be alligators and a few non-native species with a nasty temper that will thrive in this climate. It's harsh. The world was harsh, always, but we were harsher. It's time to accept the fact that we are temporary, each individual, but we have to maintain the longevity of species. Not just our species. We're a niche. We shouldn't be making the decisions because we'll always make the decision that benefits us. We're too selfish to remain unchecked."

She spent the night thinking about it. They had dinner and there was beer and everyone got a little too loud with wary eyes shifting left and right. These were people who had dedicated years of their lives to the restoration. They had understood it; they had sworn to uphold it. but now it was time to prove it.

They got quieter as the night wore on and drifted off silently to their beds. They all rose early and stood in front of Alex, in the room with the boxes.

"Anyone want a particular box?" Alex asked. "Besides the snakes?" He handed Zach that one.

Then there was silence. They all hesitated. Choice seemed somehow to suggest culpability. But she ran though her own thoughts, her own objectives, her own decisions to save the earth, no matter what. She remembered the curtain of spiders, and how awful she had felt—a terrible, consuming, destroying human reaction. She hated siders and she might as well admit it. And she should also admit that destroying what you hated was how they'd all gotten into this mess. She should turn her fears into dedication, maybe. She should really take her chances, and not rely on staying safe.

"I'll take the spiders," she sighed and stepped forward.

He nodded and gave them to her. She could hear faint skitterings in the box. There were air-holes, and she thought she saw a hairy black leg stick through a hole briefly and then subside. She took a long breath and made her way out the door.

Her heart skittered too, but her hold was firm.

Karen Heuler's stories have appeared in over 100 literary and speculative magazines and anthologies, from *Conjunctions* to *Weird Tales*, as well as a number of Best Of anthologies. She has published four novels, four collections, and a novella, and has won an O. Henry award, and been a finalist for many others.

9 781955 360005